Gods of the Desert Winds

William G. Collins

Gods of the Desert Winds

Copyright 2018 William G. Collins

ISBN-13: 978-1727753165

ISBN-10: 172775316X

This book is a work of fiction. Except for historical references, names, characters, businesses, organizations, places, events, and incidents are the product of the author's imagination or are used factiously. Any resemblance to actual persons living or dead or to locales is entirely coincidental.

Cover design: Chris Holmes: Whiterabbitgraphics.com
Interior design: Marie Brack

Books on Ancient Egypt by the Author

Murder by the Gods (book 1)
Gods of the Desert Winds (book 2)

The Egyptian Cat Mysteries:

Book 1: Murder in Pharaoh's Palace
Book 2: Death Beneath the Sphinx
Book 3: Murder at Abu Simbel

Behind the Golden Mask
In the Land of Dreams
Prince of the Nile

Visit the website: Collinsauthor.com
Or his blog:
BillLovesEgypt.wordpress.com

Acknowledgments

A special appreciation to the Florida Writers
Association Group, The Daytona Writers, led by
regional leader, author Veronica H. Hart:
Christine Holmes, Dr. Robert Hart, Marie Brack,
Dr. William Dempsey, Marie Brack, Dr. Walter
Doherty, Robert Shell, Rob Minks, and Richard Milam.
I also give special appreciation to Marie Brack
for the layout and interior design, and to Chris
Holmes of Whiterabbitgraphics.com for another
magnificent cover.

Introduction

This is a sequel to *"Murder by the Gods,"* set at the beginning of the First Dynasty in Ancient Egypt. Words we associate with Egypt do not yet exist such as *Pharaoh*, the *Nile,* or *Egypt* itself. The words we associate with the ancient great civilization, were given much later by the Greeks as their culture expanded around the Mediterranean.

Kemet, known by the people as the 'Black Land', benefited from the precious black soil carried to it by the great sacred river every year. At the time of these stories, the country has been ruled and united by King Narmer, thought by archeologists to be the Scorpion King and first of the royal families of the land. At his death, Prince Aha, his son, assumes the throne and is the central figure of the first book.

Early in his rule, King Aha learns of an evil brotherhood made up of the followers of Set, the god of darkness and the underworld. Set the destroyer. Those who worship him vow to destroy Aha and all the royal family.

The leader of the followers of Set is Cobra, who begins a systematic reign of terror against the royal family—including the murder of Aha's queen. A warrior and childhood friend, Prince Akhom, vows to hunt him down and free the land of the murderous worshippers of the evil deity. Arranging one of the king's favorites hunts in the delta, Cobra manages to place King Aha in the path of rampaging hippos who trample the king to death.

Akhom, who as the king's childhood friend and blood brother, traps Cobra in the swampy land of the delta and ends not only the assassin's life, but all the followers of Set who are arrested and eliminated.

This book begins as Aha's son, Prince Djed, king now for five years, returns to the royal burial grounds at Abydos to honor the lives of his father and mother. His long-time friend, Prince Ako, son of Akhom, travels with him and share memories of when the tomb was sealed. Something happens on their return which demonstrates only too clearly, that the evil brotherhood is still alive and has returned to threaten the king and those he loves.

*"Man, know yourself
and you shall know the gods."*

Written on the temple at Luxor

1

"Hail, Great and Glorious Aha," the young prince shouted, his eyes fixed on the falcon high above. "We honor you, Beloved Son of Ra, and Father of King Djed."

The raptor cried and began its dive. Raising his army slightly, Ko tightened the leather band on his wrist. The sacred and majestic bird spread its wings and hovered before landing on the prince's arm.

"Greetings, young god of the sky," Ako said in a soothing voice. "You have grown these years since our king was taken from us."

At sixteen summers, the young prince was slim and well-muscled, his skin a golden bronze. Black curly hair, cut short for the hottest months crowned his head. The promise of a beard shaded his jaw. He was there with the royal family who prepared to honor King Aha—killed by a murderous sect known as the followers of Set, god of darkness and the underworld. It had been five summers since the king's entombment.

A large crowd from the necropolis of Abydos waited for the tributes to begin.

Aha's son and successor, King Djer and his queen, Nakhtneith, Ko's older sister, moved to their positions for the ceremony of remembrance.

"Hail, Great Aha," the king proclaimed in a loud voice. A priest handed him a gold container of burning incense and the king lifted it into the air. "We remember and honor your name."

The crowd shouted, "We remember his name."

Ako's father, Prince Akhom, walked forward and handed a golden platter to the high priest who placed it on the altar. Sweet incense permeated the air and its scented smoke carried their prayers to the heavens.

The young prince's chest filled with pride as he stood beside his father. Akhom and the departed king grew up together, and when an assassin murdered the king on a hunt, it was Akhom who caught and killed the murderer. This was their fifth visit to Aha's tomb. Each year, after the celebrations for the inundation of the sacred river, the royal family accompanied Aha's son, King Hor-Djer to the royal tomb.

Gifts to the god were presented by family members as a deep-voiced chorus of priests sang hymns to Horus-Ra—god of the sun and protector of the royal family.

On board the royal galley, a great feast awaited them. The king and queen changed into comfortable clothes, as did the rest of the family. The Breath of Horus remained at anchor in the harbor, allowing the royal children to run free across the deck under the watchful eye of servants and guardians.

When the food was in place on two large tables, the king invited Ako's father to sit with them on the royal platform. His invitation included Lady Nafrini, his wife, and their son, Ako, simply called Ko.

The Queen Mother, Lady Khenthap, widow of the late king, sat in an honored place at the table next to her son.

Akhom addressed the king. "It seems like only yesterday, Majesty. Five years ago, I stood outside the tomb and saw your father's Ka—that part of us that never dies—fly up on the wings of a falcon into the heavens. This I swear upon my life, Majesty."

Everyone on deck chanted, "We remember his glory."

"I remember that moment, too, Uncle," the king said. "You were standing on the highest dune, and I saw you look up as they flew higher. It was the god Horus' blessing, and I was thrilled by the sight." The king's shaved head glistened in the sunlight. His square jaw proved he was his father's son. He refused to wear any of the kohl eyeliner or shadow. Several gold necklaces covered his bare chest.

Ko's sister, the queen, smiled. "No king could have had a better brother or friend than you, Father."

The now elderly Queen Mother spoke in a quiet voice, "We are pleased you and your family have come with us again, Lord Akhom."

Young crown prince Djet interrupted. "Father, will you play hounds and jackals with me after the feast? I am going to win this time."

The king gave out a deep belly laugh. "Never. Why would I let a young lion cub beat the Great Lion?"

Prince Djet laughed. Having lived through eighteen summers, he was tall and put his hands on his hips as he'd seen his father do when angry. "You are too old, Majesty. Your reactions are slow."

Ko looked at his sister, the queen, and grinned.

She laughed and shook her head. "Beware, my Husband. You have a son eager to tame the Great Lion."

Djet, everyone simply called Jet, said, "You see. Even the queen knows you are in danger."

The king motioned for the servants to bring in the food. Large platters of roasted antelope and beef were placed on the tables. Steamed leeks, green beans and other vegetables as well as a variety of fruit covered the tables. Servants filled the royal cups with wine repeatedly.

When they finished, the king waved his hand and a servant ran into the cabin to bring the game board. He placed it and the play-pieces on a small table, and brought chairs for father and son.

Ko watched them begin, but then walked to the railing of the ship and inhaled the wonderful fragrances of the river—lotus blossoms, lush green vegetation and the heavy perfume of blue water hyacinths. He was tall like his father who had given him his nose and chin, but his large hazel eyes were a gift from his mother.

It was wonderful evening, and to Ko, the royal family seemed no different than other folk along the river. He chose not to sleep in one of the ship's cabins, but preferred lying on plush cushions on deck in front of his parents' cabin.

Early the next morning, Ko rolled up his comforter and walked to the railing. He leaned over it as the crew tossed raised the anchors and the great ship left sailed south against the current. The capital city of Memphis was but a day away.

His father came up behind him. "What are you thinking, my Son?"

Ko didn't turn around, but continued to gaze at the passing landscape. "I was thinking how proud I am to have such a brave father. You captured King Aha's killer and stopped the sons of Set."

His father remained silent for a moment. "But I could not save him from those hippos. The killer struck him down and threw him in front of the beasts to be trampled to death." A dark shadow seemed to touch his eyes and he sighed. "I shudder even now when I think of it. Aha feared hippos his whole life. To see him killed like that by those beasts haunts me every day."

Ko turned around. "You are still a hero to me, my Lord, and to the king's family. They honor you for finding his killer."

Akhom put his hand on his son's shoulder. "Honor me by doing well at the army training garrison. I respect you for having the courage to follow your dream. It is what you've always wanted."

Ko put his foot up on the rope railing. "Prince Djet is one summer older than me. He never lets me forget it. Perhaps I can prove his equal at the academy."

Ahead of the ship, a bloat of hippos jumped up and down like water horses in the center of the river. "Your cousin may have survived one more summer than you, but he needs military training if he is to succeed his father one day. He may be older, but what he needs now is someone to be his friend and protect him."

Ko nodded. "I like him and I am glad he is coming too." He turned back and looked toward the bow where the king's daughter Merneith, two summers younger than he, amused herself by painting on pieces of papyrus. Almost a woman, her beauty reflected her mother's features. She waved to him and he waved back. Two maidservants sat on cushions near her.

His father said, "I am going to join your mother in the shade of the king's awning."

"I will be along shortly," Ko replied. He frowned at several crocodiles that slid off the riverbank into the water, their large jaws opening and closing as if in anticipation of some unsuspecting meal.

Splashing below caused him to look down at a canoe rushing past in the opposite direction. It came close to the ship, but he thought nothing of it. When he turned back to the bow expecting to see the princess, she was gone. Her paintbrushes lay scattered on deck. Ako thought she must have retired to the royal cabin with her attendants.

He walked toward the cabins astern. "Mother, have you seen Merry?"

"Yes. She is painting on deck with her guardians."

"No, she is not there. I think I had better check on her." He walked forward and found Jet. "Where is your sister, Highness?"

The young royal grumbled, "I am not in charge of her, Ko. You know that."

"Yes, Prince, but I cannot find her. She was playing over there with her paintbrushes, but she's gone. Help me find her."

"Oh, very well, she is always getting into trouble. Girls—they are all alike."

Ko and Jet looked everywhere including the hold, but without success.

"You'd better tell the king," Ko said. "I'll come with you."

The prince nodded and led the way to the special deck where the king and queen relaxed on soft cushioned divans.

"Father, forgive the intrusion, but we cannot find Merry. She is not on the ship."

"What? Guards!" the king shouted.

Royal guardsmen rushed to the royal deck. "Search the ship," the king ordered. "The Princess is missing!"

"No one has seen her attendants either, Great One," Ko said.

Manu, the ship's captain rushed to the king's side. "What is it, Majesty?"

"Search the ship, Captain. My daughter is gone. I will throw you and your crew into the river if she is not found."

"Majesty," was all Manu could say as he rushed back to the helm. "Furl the sail and throw out the anchors." He grabbed his first mate by the shoulders. "Princess Merry is missing. Search wherever a child could hide."

Ko walked along the deck toward the helm where the rudder men sat on benches, relieved the ship had stopped. When he gripped the railing, his hand felt a rope attached to it and then found another. Leaning over the side, he discovered a rope ladder hanging from them. He climbed over and then down it. Halfway to the water, he found a piece of blue cloth caught on a rope. Attached to the ladder he removed a rolled-up papyrus scroll tied to the ladder. Thrusting it into the belt of his kilt, he hurried back up. On deck, he opened the scroll and read:

"The princess is unharmed.

500 deben of gold will free her.

Wait for instructions."

There was no signature—only a symbol that made Ko's blood turn cold. At the bottom, using what looked like blood, was the glyph for the sign of Set, god of darkness.

"Gods, no," Ko swore as he ran toward the king's cabin.

The king shouted to servants and staff, "How could this happen? I will have every one of you torn to pieces!"

The queen wept into her hands as Ko approached her. "Sister, do you recognize this blue cloth?"

Nakhneith raised her head, examined the cloth and cried, "It is Merry's robe. Oh, no."

The king walked over. "Show me."

"It is from Merry's robe, Majesty. The rope of a ladder thrown over the side snagged it. I saw a canoe row past us in the opposite direction with three or four people in it. They must have taken her and left the message."

The king opened it, read the message and collapsed onto his divan. "God's no! Not this curse again. First my father and mother, and now me. I swear before Horus and our Father Ra that I will drive these Sons of Set from our land like the vermin they are!"

He showed the scroll to his queen and in a soothing voice said, "They will not harm her, my Love. Go inside and rest. I assure you we will bring her back to you."

The queen nodded, squeezed his hand, and allowed her attendants to lead her inside the royal cabin.

Captain Bakaa of the King's Guards took Ko aside. "Show me the rope ladder."

Ko led him to the starboard side and showed him where the ropes had been attached.

"How can they do this in plain daylight, Ko? Someone must have seen them."

"I don't know, Captain. I believe her two attendants must be behind it. The princess would go with them because she has trusted them ever since she was little."

"Agreed, but wouldn't the crew have seen a canoe coming that near the ship?"

Captain Manu approached and overheard the captain's question. "Not always, Captain. Canoes pass us all the time. I'm sure no one thought anything of it."

"We need a map, Captain. They've probably gone into hiding near here."

"In my cabin," Manu said. "Follow me."

Ko noticed Manu sweating profusely. It wasn't from the heat, but he knew the man feared for his life and those of his crew.

"Help us, Bakaa," Manu said, when he closed the door. "Please. We did not do this."

Bakaa shook his head. "Calm yourself. We are trying to find out what happened. Give us a map of the river and help us locate the village closest to where we've stopped."

Manu unrolled one of his many maps and spread it out across the table. "Here's where we are, at this large bend." He then pointed to a red circle. "This is the village of Ipu, or some call it Khent-min. It's the closest."

Ko brushed a fly away from his face. "Would they be able to hide a royal princess in such a small village, Captain?"

The officer frowned. "I doubt it. We are near Thinis, the old capital, and people know the royal family very well. They love them. Someone would recognize Princess Merneith, and remember, all royal children have the king's mark on the back of their neck."

Ko nodded, and subconsciously touched the tattoo on his neck.

Bakaa said, "Couldn't they hide her somewhere in the desert?"

Manu pulled on his goatee. "I don't know the land as well as the river, but I have heard there are caves in the desert, south of town."

Captain Bakaa commanded, "Turn this ship around and put us ashore, Captain. I'll leave half of my men here to guard the king and the rest will come with me. We'll need our horses, of course."

Ko interrupted. "You'd better tell his majesty."

"Of course, son," Bakaa responded as he left the cabin.

The prince frowned. He didn't like people reminding him of his age but followed the officer to the king's cabin.

When the king heard Bakaa's plan he said. "Good. I will lead you, Captain."

"Of course," Bakaa said, kneeling and striking his chest with his fist.

Ko objected. "Majesty, I know we are not permitted to tell you what to do, but as your nephew, Uncle, do not do this. Your people need you and so does your family. Let the Captain and your guards find Merry. Please, Mighty Bald One."

Captain Bakaa grimaced at Ko's crude insult.

But the king smiled. It was what Ko's father called Djer's father. Being king meant having to shave one's head.

The king placed his hand on the young man's shoulder. "Very well, Ko. Bring her back to me and take your father with you."

Inside the cave, Kiya growled, "Keep her quiet."

Nani held Princess Merneith's hand. "Quiet dear one. No one is going to harm you."

"Take me home," the girl sobbed. "I order you to obey me."

Her servants laughed. They had dressed her in rags and covered her heard with a dark-brown cloth to cover the girl's neck.

Kiya snarled, "Do you want me to tie your mouth closed again?"

The princess shook her head. Tears ran down her cheeks but she stopped sobbing.

"Now be quiet."

The two men who rowed the canoe entered the cave.

Merry cringed at the sight of the larger man. He was dark-skinned, had a large curved nose like some evil bird, and had already squeezed her arm too tightly.

"I don't believe the king will pay the ransom, Sitka," he said.

The other man was smaller and younger, the princess thought.

"He'll pay. His father remembers what our great leader, Cobra, did to Aha's family."

"Quiet, you two," Kiya grumbled. "Did you bring the food?"

"Here it is, you old hag. Caring for babies was not part of this. We were to capture the princess and bring her here. That's all."

Kiya was tall and solidly built and the princess could sense that the men were afraid of her. She, however, had always been loving and kind to the girl could not understand why she was doing this. Why would she allow the others to treat the king's daughter in such a bad way?

Kiya crossed her arms. "I'm in charge here, and Stau will not be pleased if you make it difficult for us."

The princess moved closer to Nani and closed her eyes.

"It will soon be over," Nani said. "Your father will pay the gold and you will go home."

"Who are these people?" Merry asked.

"It is best you don't know, Highness."

"Take your bread and go stand guard," Kiya ordered the men.

They grumbled to each other but did as ordered.

Merry must have fallen asleep, because when she opened her eyes the outside of the cave was colored red by the setting sun. A fire burned in the cave and she moved closer to it. Approaching hoof beats came to a halt outside, and several men walked into the nearly dark chamber.

"Where is she?" a large heavy-set man demanded.

Kiya stood and put herself between the man and the princess "She is here, Stau. You are not to harm her or the servants of Set will make you pay."

"Stand aside, woman. I want to make sure it is the princess."

Kiya turned around and took the princess's hand. "Show him your neck, child."

The princess pulled aside her long raven-black hair and the brown cloth so the man could see the king's mark of the royal name.

"So, this is the granddaughter of Aha, the evil and now dead king. If I had my way, they would all be dead."

Kiya pushed him back toward the entrance. "Then it's a good thing you won't have your way. Our leaders have plans for the gold she can bring. They are planning to end the reign of the sons of Horus. Now be gone if you're satisfied it is the princess."

"I am, and I wouldn't stay another moment in your company you troublesome hag of a woman. I pray Set's curse on you, but from the looks of you, that has already happened." He burst out laughing, motioning to the other men who followed him out of the cave.

"I do not like it here, Nani. I want to go home," the princess whispered.

"Shh, we're going to eat something and I'll tell you a story. You'd like that wouldn't you?"

Merry nodded.

Nani took a small clay jar the men brought and puts a spoonful of honey on the bread and handed it to the princess. "Now let me tell you the story about our Mother Isis and the stupid monkey."

When the girl fell asleep, Kiya said, "I think we should get out of here. We can't trust Stau—I feel it in my bones. We can go on foot while it is dark. I have a long knife to protect us."

Nani's voice trembled. "Where will we go?"

"Into the red lands. The gods of the desert winds will protect us." She walked to the cave entrance and waited until the men's fire burned low.

Nani slipped away first, and a few moments later, Kiya picked up the princess, threw her over her shoulder, and disappeared into the darkness.

2

Captain Bakaa stopped his men on the edge of the village. "Spread out and search every house and farm. Offer rewards if need be. Look for anything out of the ordinary. Meet in the center of town when you hear the trumpet. These assassins must have left a trail—find it."

Ko and his father rode with the guards and reined in their horses at the home of the mayor.

At the arrival of so many soldiers, the mayor awaited them. When he saw the thin gold bands encircling the visitor's heads, he prostrated himself. "Welcome, Highness. Your presence honors us. I am Ibebi, mayor of Ipu."

"Thank you, Lord Ibebi. We are here on the king's business."

"Enter Noble Ones. Come out of the sun."

Ko's eyes took a moment to adjust to the welcome shade of the house. When the mayor offered chairs, his father raised his hand.

"We have no time, Lord Mayor. The king's daughter is missing, taken by assassins, and we believe they brought her to your village. The king's guards are searching every dwelling and shop. We must find the princess or all our lives will be in jeopardy."

The look of horror on Ibebi's face showed genuine shock. Ko turned his head as a young woman entered with a pitcher of water.

"Oh, you looking for Princess Merry?" she asked.

Ko said, "Yes. Have you seen her these past two days?"

The woman shook her head. "No, there would be crowds of children around her if she were here. Everyone loves her. She speaks our dialect so well."

The mayor waved the woman away.

Prince Akhom asked, "Are there any places for people to hide—you know, troublemakers, or perhaps those who don't like to obey the king's laws?"

"Not here, Highness. But up in the desert hills of the Lizard's Back, there are caves. They are good hiding places because there is a spring nearby. When someone has a fire, their families often take refuge in them until their homes can be rebuilt."

"Lizard's Back?" Ko repeated.

"Yes. From a distance the hills resemble the spikes of the horned lizard."

"Thank you, my Lord," Akhom said. "We'll go there at once. I pray the blessing of King Djer on this house."

"We remember the name of his father, the Great Aha," Ibebi said, bowing his head slightly.

Ko and his father left the house and climbed back on their horses. Heading directly for the center of town, they dismounted and tied up their animals near the well. Captain Bakaa arrived shortly after, jumped down from his horse and approached them.

"Anything, Highness?"

The prince nodded. "We have learned about caves at Lizard's Back. We need to head there now. Call your men."

Bakaa whistled several times and his aide rode into the square. "Signal the men."

The sergeant saluted, removed a small animal horn attached to his saddle, and blew the signal for assembly. A few moments later, he blew it again. The first guards arrived followed by the rest of the company.

"Wait a moment, Father," Ko said. He jumped onto his horse and rode back to the mayor's house. The official rushed out to see what was wrong.

"We need someone to take us there, my Lord."

"Yes, of course." He turned, entered the house, shouted someone's name and in a moment returned with a young boy of perhaps eight summers or nine. "Take my grandson. He knows the way."

"Good." Ko leaned over and extended his hand to the boy, who grabbed it. Ko pulled him up and the boy sat behind him. Kicking his horse in the flanks, they galloped back to the center of town. "We needed a guide, Father."

"Excellent thinking. Lead on."

"Tell me the way, boy," Ko said. "How are you called?"

"I am Pepy," the boy shouted above the pounding of the horse's hooves. "You must turn here at the big rock," and he pointed to a small trail leading out into the desert.

Sweat began to run down the middle of Ko's back. He hoped it wouldn't be far to the caves. His thick short hair didn't give as much protection from the sun as he would have liked. His throat had become parched.

At the top of a small sandy hill, Pepy pointed to the right. "There, my Lord."

Ko saw the long formation of cliffs not too far distant. A blue smoky haze hung over them, poking up from the sand like the back of a lizard.

Captain Bakaa sent a scout on ahead and the man returned in good time. Taking a moment to catch his breath he said, "There are two horses there, Captain. It must be them."

Bakaa called a halt and then consulted with Ko's father. "We don't want to scare them away. I recommend we dismount and continue on foot."

"Agreed," Akhom said. "We are still a good distance away. We need to keep low."

"Yes, Highness. I also recommend we divide into two squads and approach them as scorpion's pincers. One unit on the left the other to the right."

Bakaa's sergeant passed the word to the men, who split up. He told them to move fast and as silently as possible. "Move out," he ordered. Two guards stayed with the horses, tying them to several large thorn acacias.

Ko and his father moved toward the cliffs while the captain led the second group. Several times, they crouched down at the top of small rises in the sand so as not to become silhouettes. Ko breathed in the dry dusty smell of the desert and ran his tongue over his lips.

After a short time, the captain raised his arm and whispered, "They are at the well in front of the cave. There seems to be only the two of them." He whistled the call of the desert thrush, and the archers from the left squad fired arrows into the sand close to the two men as a warning. Bakaa's group moved around and blocked the entrance to the cave.

The guards rushed the two men who offered no resistance, forcing them to the ground threw them on the ground and disarming them. Several men hurried into the cave but returned quickly. "There's no one here, Captain."

"Where is she?" Akhom shouted. "Where is the princess?"

"We don't know," one of the men shouted. "We only stopped here for water."

Bakaa shouted, "Tie them up, we'll throw them into the river as an offering to Sobek."

"Mercy, Captain," the other man shouted. "All right. We were asked to bring food to the cave, that's all."

Akhom took Bakaa and Ko aside. "They're lying, Captain. Why bring food? For what purpose? The mayor would have told us if there was a family staying here, or anyone else. Merchants wouldn't stay here. It's too close to town."

"I agree, Highness. I'll get the truth out of them."

"If they are the kidnappers, tie them up and don't treat them kindly," Ko said.

Bakaa nodded and then walked back to the well.

Ko asked for one of the guards to start a fire so he could make a torch. "I want to look inside the cave, Aiutu."

Prince Akhom nodded.

Carrying a burning branch of acacia, he entered the cave. Bats flew out as smoke reached them on the ceiling. He looked on the ground carefully for any trace of Merry's presence, but there was nothing. As he was about to turn and leave, something on the wall caught his eye. There were scratch marks made by people who had stayed in the cave, but one was different. He ran outside and shouted, "Aiutu, Father! Come see."

Akhom and Bakaa rushed in and Ko held the torch closer.

His father shouted, "She was here. Smart girl. She's written the king's name and put the royal cartouche around it."

Captain Bakaa growled. "What have they done with her?" He spat on the ground. "Well, we'll soon find out." He hurried outside and kicked one of the prisoners. "Where is she? She was here and left her mark. You are dead men."

"Not us, Captain. If we tell you who has taken her, will you spare us? We only brought them food."

"Traitor," the other man shouted. "Keep quiet."

Ko studied them carefully and had to resist the urge to kill them. Then he saw the mark. "Look on their necks, Captain," he shouted.

Bakaa leaned closer and swore, "By the gods. The mark of Set."

"What have you done with her?" Akhom shouted. He leaned over and struck the closest prisoner on the face. "Foul scum. Now, you will not live."

The first prisoner trembled. "Mercy, Lords. It was the two women who took her."

"Shut up, Shai—you son of a jackal," his companion shouted.

"Women?" Bakaa repeated.

Ko said, "Do you mean Nani and Kiya, her attendants?"

The man nodded his head rapidly. "They left with her before we could come back with more food. We don't know where they've gone."

Bakaa walked some distance from the well scratching his head. Akhom and Ko followed.

"These spawn of Set," the officer swore. "They could have gone anywhere."

"Maybe not, Captain," Akhom said. "If they have no horses they can't have gone far—especially in this heat. Let's ask the boy if he knows where someone might go and in what direction. You have excellent trackers. Follow their trail while it is light."

Bakaa nodded, called for his sergeant, and explained what they wanted to do.

One of his men shouted, "Here are their tracks, Captain. There were three of them. Their footprints are fresh."

The soldiers cheered.

"Fill your canteens, Captain," Ko said. "Send a couple of men to bring our horses and we can make better time."

"Please, Nani, I can't go on," Merry gasped, out of breath.

"We've got to keep moving. Here, have some water," Nani said.

Kiya growled. "Stop that. That's all the water we have until we reach the river."

"It will be dark soon, Kiya. Jackals will hunt us and that will be the end."

The princess said, "Please. I can't walk anymore."

"Very well, my precious lady. We'll just leave you here."

Nani raised her voice. "No, we won't, Kiya. What we've done is bad enough. The goddess Maat will judge us more severely for her death."

"Maat? Hah! You don't believe those tales do you?"

Nani stopped talking. There was nothing more important than to attain the balance of Maat in one's life. If things were not made right, the Ka—the eternal part of a person, would die and go to dwell in Set's underworld. A shudder ran down her spine. She put her arm around the princess and helped her along the trail. "How much farther is it?"

Kiya growled, "Don't ask stupid questions. How do I know? Sitka said it was in this direction. Now move on."

Nani had seen the princess cut the royal name into the wall of the cave but didn't say anything. She secretly hoped the king's men would find them before harm came to her royal ward. She had been with the princess for fourteen summers now and loved taking care of her. Why had she allowed Kiya to talk her into the abduction? She was not a bad person and if caught, the dishonor would affect her family back in the village. Perhaps once they reached the river they could take Merry to a safer place to await the ransom.

Suddenly something bit her leg and she cried out.

"What is it now, Nani?" the older woman shouted.

"A serpent bit me and it stings like fire."

Merry backed away as a viper slithered off the path and into the scrub bushes.

"Come, Merry," Kiya said. "Leave her there."

The princess shook her head. "No, we must take care of her. I love her."

"She's already dead. No one can survive a viper's bite. The gods have punished her."

"Don't leave me," Nani gasped, already finding it hard to breathe.

Merry broke away from Kiya and knelt beside the kind woman. She kissed her on the cheek and put an arm around her.

Nani began to lose her vision. "Help me," she whispered, her head fell back and everything went black.

Captain Bakaa's trackers were having an easy time following the footprints in the sand. Each of the captain's guards led their horses by the reins. The animals carried extra canteens of water. The trackers rushed ahead and changed directions several times until the head tracker approached the captain.

"They're headed for the river, Captain."

"Then we must intercept them before they get there. If they were to take another ship, we would never be able to follow them. Horus help us," Akhom said.

"Agreed, Highness," Bakaa said. "You trackers must go faster."

The man saluted, fist to chest, and ran on ahead to join the others.

A shout from the farthest tracker made everyone rush ahead.

"Now there are only two," Bakaa said as he turned over the body of Nani. "The gods have taken their revenge."

Ko swallowed hard. He knew Nani well and while angry for what she did, regretted her death. "Her family will starve," he told his father. "The money she sent home kept them alive. She has five small brothers and sisters. Why would she get involved in this?"

Lord Akhom said, "I fear for the princess, Son. If there is one viper on the trail, there are others. Be vigilant everyone."

Bakaa said, "It will soon be dark. What a foolish woman."

"He's right," Ko said. "Let's ride on ahead at a faster pace. We may be able to reach them before the sun sets."

Captain Bakaa said, "And I will ride with you, Prince."

Ko mounted his horse and dug in his heels, urging it into a gallop.

Bakaa rode behind and they soon passed the trackers.

"The path is well-worn, Captain. Just follow the trail," a tracker shouted as they rode past.

Ko touched the short sword attached to his belt. If there were jackals around, they would need weapons.

"Can you still see their tracks, Ko?"

"Yes, their prints are clear," the prince encouraged his steed forward. As they crested the next small hill, he shouted, "There she is." He kicked in his heels and his horse ran faster with Bakaa right behind.

The princess shouted "Ko. . . help me!"

The young man reined in his horse and jumped to the ground.

"Stay away," Kiya yelled.

Ko stopped when he saw the long knife held against the princess' neck.

"I'll slit her throat. Back away if you want her to live."

Bakaa growled. "You don't have a chance, Kiya. Everyone knows who you are and what you have done. The king will not allow you to live. You have violated the royal person."

Ko slowly moved closer as the captain talked. If he could get behind the woman, he could grab the princess from her arms.

Kiya turned the princess around and pushed her ahead along the trail. She kept turning her head to keep an eye on the two men. "I'm warning you both. Keep your distance."

Bakaa glanced at Ko and nodded. They would have to wait for the right moment to get closer.

In the dusk, it became harder to see and the tall woman stumbled several times over roots and rocks.

Ko shouted, "Let her go. We won't follow you, Kiya. You can make it to the river on your own and get away."

Bakaa was about to object, but Ko whispered, "She'll never make it, sir. Jackals will make a quick meal of her."

The woman stopped.

"You can use your long knife to fight off any wild animals up ahead, but leave the princess I beg you. Don't do this," Ko said.

"The gods curse you," Kiya shouted. She shoved the princess to the ground and ran on ahead.

Ko rushed to Merry, helped her up and held her in his arms.

Bakaa jumped down and hurried over. "Is she all right? Has she been cut anywhere?"

The prince shook his head. "No, only a few scratches on her legs and arms. Thank the gods."

By then, his father and the trackers reached them and cheered the fact that they had found the princess alive and well.

Akhom put his hand on his son's shoulder. "You and Bakaa have done well."

Ko poured water from his canteen over the princess' face. She tightened her grip around his neck and opened her eyes.

"Ko, you did it. You saved me."

"Well, Captain Bakaa was with me."

"Yes, I know. But I was praying you'd rescue me. Just you—and you did."

"Drink this, Princess," Ko's father said, handing her his waterskin.

She drank for the longest time and then handed it back. "Now," she said, "I order you guards of my father's regiment to take me home."

The men laughed and clapped their hands at her bravery. She appeared to have a clear grasp of what had happened and whose daughter she was.

In the distance, a troop of jackals howled and a loud human scream broke the desert silence.

Ko shook his head. "Kiya didn't make it to the river."

Helping the princess onto his horse, he said, "Now let's go home."

He felt Merry's arms around his waist, and silently thanked the gods she was all right.

3

In the royal city of Memphis, the gold and silver trim of the large Hall of Audiences welcomed the courtiers who entered and stood on either side of a long aisle leading to two thrones. A polished limestone floor reflected the colors of paintings depicting royal exploits on the walls and ceiling. Savory aromas drifted into the great hall from next door. A feast had been prepared to celebrate the return of the king's daughter and savory aromas wafted into the great hall.

A short flourish of trumpets caused the invited guests to turn toward the entrance as Prince Ako walked in holding the hand of Princess Merneith. Everyone bowed low as the royals passed. He smiled because she had refused to walk with her brother, Jet, the Crown Prince, and insisted he escort her. She was almost as tall as him and she wore a floor-length light-blue gown. Pinned up with golden brooches, her auburn hair made her appear even taller. A beautiful emerald necklace matching the color of her eyes encircled her neck.

Ko couldn't believe how much she'd changed from the gangly child he knew. At fourteen summers, she was becoming a beautiful young woman.

Suddenly, Merry whispered, "Oh, no, there's Lord Baky, that old hippo. Who invited him?"

Ko squeezed her hand and whispered, "Keep your eyes straight ahead, Highness. He can't help it if he looks like one."

She chuckled and squeezed back. "Ah," she whispered, ignoring his instructions, "now there's a lady for you, Cousin. Lady Neferu—look how you make her cheeks flush at the sight of you."

"Behave, Merry."

At the first step leading up to the royal dais, he let her walk to the royal thrones and take her place beside her mother. Ko turned, and walked to his place next to his parents.

Another brief flourish of trumpets announced the entrance of Prince Djet, heir to the throne. He held his head high as he joined his sister, but stood on the right, next to his father's throne.

A much longer and louder fanfare of trumpets announced the entrance of their majesties. This time the courtiers prostrated themselves, they turned toward the king. When King Djed and his queen reached the steps, he escorted his wife to her throne. He then embraced his daughter affectionately and turned to face the court.

"We welcome the safe return of our beloved Merneith, and invite you, dear friends, to join us for a feast of celebration in the banquet hall. We will honor her and those who rescued her."

The courtiers clapped and shouted the princess' name—"Mer-neith! Mer-neith!"

The king then took his daughter's hand on his left, the queen on his right, and escorted them into the banquet hall.

The crown prince walked behind them, and Ko followed him. He then walked to his place at his mother and father's table.

Today, for this special occasion, the young princess sat on the king's right—a special place of honor.

The king signaled to the musicians who began playing soft music with harps, sistrums and small drums.

Ko inhaled the wonderful aromas of roasted gazelle, geese and peacock. Surrounding these delicacies were heaping platters of leeks, radishes, choriander, beans, and cabbage. Bowls of melons and yellow apples were set at the ends of the tables.

"You have honored our family, Son," his father said looking straight ahead. "You and Bakaa saved Merry and will be blessed by the gods."

His son smiled. "And you were there, Father. We could not have done it without you. But I still have a question."

"Oh?"

"Yes. Since the followers of Set did not receive their gold ransom, won't they try again?"

His father sipped his wine and then cleared his throat. There were wisps of grey in his hair now that Ko hadn't noticed before, and small wrinkles around the eyes. "Bakaa has asked me the same question. I told him what I am telling you now. The king and I were certain five years ago that the followers of the foul Cobra who killed King Aha were all destroyed." He turned to look at his son. "It is evident they were not. We are certain they will try again, but we will talk of this further at another time."

"Of course."

As the celebratory meal continued, an additional parade of platters filled with delicacies from the south were brought in. Flowers of every kind added their fragrances to the wonderful ambiance of the ornate Hall.

When it ended, Lord Ankhkahf, the chamberlain, struck the floor with his long staff three times. In his deep strong voice, he proclaimed, "Hear our great King and Father of the Land, Hor-Djer, Son of Ra, heir to King Aha, may his name live forever."

The courtiers chorused, "Long life to the king!"

A respectful silence filled the room as the king stood. "We honor three persons today. The first is Her Highness, Princess Merneith, our beloved daughter."

The courtiers shouted her name and clapped their hands.

The king lifted his hand, palm toward them, and the room fell silent. "We honor also, members of the Royal Guards who rescued her."

More applause echoed around the room.

"Captain Bakaa, stand forth," the king ordered.

Ko smiled as the captain, who had been standing with his men at the back, walked forward. Before the king's table, he knelt on one knee and struck his fist against his chest.

His majesty walked down the steps and stood in front of Bakaa. The chamberlain joined him carrying a thin cedar box.

"Stand, Captain," the king ordered, and Bakaa did so.

The chamberlain opened the box and the king took out a gold necklace on which a small gold bar was suspended. The king's throne name was engraved on it worth one deben—the salary of a soldier for one year.

The king continued. "We honor you by giving you this Gold of Valor for saving Princess Merneith, and for your bravery at the risk of your own life." He turned the captain around to face the people.

The courtiers chanted his name, "Ba-kaa. Ba-kaa."

The king nodded to the chamberlain who struck the floor once again three times.

"His Majesty calls Prince Ako, son of His Highness Lord Akhom, to stand forth," the elderly man declared.

Surprised, Ko stood and swallowed hard. He felt his face flush and he concentrated on just walking to the front. As a royal, he simply bowed his head to the king.

King Djer addressed the court. "We honor Prince Ako, the son of my father's brother and friend, for risking his life in the rescue of our beloved Mereneith."

The court cheered and clapped with enthusiasm.

The chamberlain brought something covered by a red cloth which the king removed. He held up a gleaming silver sword which caught the light and Ko sucked in his breath.

The courtiers pounded the tables with the flat of their hands, expressing their approval of such an honor.

Lord Ankhkahf tapped his staff for silence.

"Ko," the king began, "we are proud to honor you for your courage. We give you this sword as a reminder of our gratitude and order you to report to the Military Academy at Awen for officer-training." He handed the sword to the young man who raised it high above his head.

There were more cheers and shouts of Ko's name who lowered the sword as they chanted his name over and over until he returned to his place.

Princess Merry hurried over and hugged him to the delight of everyone.

The chamberlain raised his hand, and a fanfare of trumpets signaled the departure of their majesties. The courtiers once again fell face down until the king and queen left the Hal.

Ko's father stood next to him admiring the sword. "This is a beautiful weapon, look at it. It even has your name engraved on it."

"I pray the gods will help me be a good soldier, my Lord."

'You will be," Akhom said, his voice breaking.

It had been a month since the royal banquet. Ko rode his horse Shu, god of the winds, to the royal docks. Dismounting, he handed the reins to one of the guards. Looking down at the water, he saw a solemn face—but his sixteen summers had been kind to him. Bare-chested like all soldiers, he wore two wide bands of gold around his biceps. His muscles had grown more defined and he was proud to wear the white linen warrior's kilt for the first time. As a prince of the realm, he adjusted the thin narrow gold crown on his head.

A sudden commotion made him turn away from the river. A golden carrying-chair approached and he stepped back. Thin linen curtains flew open and Princess Merry stepped out.

Ko politely bowed his head to her.

"Oh, Cousin. I couldn't let you go without saying farewell."

The prince smiled and chuckled a little. "Merry, we said our farewells at the palace last night."

"I know," she said, "but I wanted to watch you leave. Don't be angry with me."

"You know I could never be angry with you, Princess. Thank you for coming. Now where's your brother? The crew are anxious to leave."

"Don't worry, he'll be here. They were saddling his horse when I left. Take care of the big baboon for me. I'll be glad when he's not around to tease me."

Ko laughed. "You'll miss him, Merry. You like the teasing, but will never admit it." He noticed Captain Bakaa was already on board and said, "I must go, but I like that you came."

"Where are your parents?" she asked.

"We said our good byes at home."

"Oh." She paused and then said, "Wait, I almost forgot." She rushed to the carrying-chair, reached inside and returned with something. "I want you to wear this, Ko, to remember me."

She gave him a thin gold necklace with a small medallion.

He bowed so she could put it over his head. He lifted the medallion to examine it and was pleased to discover the beautifully carved image of Horus the falcon.

"It's very generous, Merry. You should not have given me a gift. I have nothing for you."

She tapped him on the shoulder. "You're leaving, Cousin. People who leave don't give gifts. I'm glad you like it. I told the royal goldsmith what I wanted. I pray Horus will protect you. Think of me when you wear it."

"I will," he said, adjusting the chain around his neck.

She motioned for him to come closer, then pulled his head down and kissed him on the cheek.

"Until we meet again," he said, kissing her on the forehead.

The hoof beats of a black stallion interrupted them. The crown prince had arrived in a commotion of servants and guards.

"The baboon has arrived," Merry grumbled, climbing back into her carrying chair.

Ko grinned. "He could have your head for insulting the Crown Prince."

"He will never be the king if I tell the world what I know about him."

Ko chuckled again and then waved to her as he walked up the gangway.

On deck, he glanced at the enormous rectangular sail still tied to the long spar high above the deck. Ropes stretched everywhere as he climbed the steps to the royal deck. The Wings of Horus was a magnificent vessel. The smell of new ropes that held the wooden planks together, was pleasing. To make them watertight, pitch helped hold them together. The crew of fifty sailors and rowers were at their posts awaiting the signal to shove off.

Prince Djet climbed the steps to the elevated platform in front of the royal cabin. He collapsed onto one of the divans on deck. "So, Cousin, was my sister pestering you?"

"Merry came to give me a parting gift," Ko said, holding out the medallion.

"You'd better watch out, that little badger is up to something."

"Do you let her call you a baboon?"

Jet guffawed. "Yes, and I love it. Baboons and badgers—that is what we are."

The king's son was about the same size and build as he. His shaved head allowed his princely braid to fall free on the right side. Ko was tempted to tease him about being the Great Bald One, but thought better of it. Jet also had a small dark birthmark on his chin the size of a fingernail. A princely goatee would eventually cover it. A large gold necklace with a medallion of Horus with outspread wings covered his bare chest. But unlike most members of the royal family, he was barefoot.

"I'm glad you are also coming to the Academy, Highness."

"First, Ko, let us agree in private to do away with titles and formalities. To you, I'm Jet, do we understand each other?"

"Of course, Prince. . . Jet. I'm sorry. It is going to take getting used to."

On shore, the prince's servants left the dock leading his horse.

"Cast off all lines," the ship's captain shouted. "Prepare to lower the sail."

Ko stood at the lower railing and his eyes grew bigger as the great sail unfurled. The huge image of the falcon god, now exposed, sparkled in the morning light as sun bounced off the golden thread of its wings. The sounds of the crew, busy at their assigned tasks made the vessel appear to be a great creature stretching and flexing its muscles. The wind filled the canvas, and Ko held on to the railing as the ship moved forward into the mainstream of the river.

Jet stood beside him. "And now the adventure begins."

In the ancient city of Thinis, former capital of the upper lands, a small band of men made their way down a passage under an abandoned temple on the edge of town. They were ordinary-looking men from various walks of life. Twenty in number, they met in a large chamber which once made up a part of the building's foundation.

The old shrine honored the god of evil, chaos and storms. Only the king and priests of Set were allowed inside and were required to undergo ritual purification in a deep stone pool. Washing was required before entering the inner sanctum of the temple.

"Where is Setmena?" one of them asked.

"He's with the priest and will be down shortly. He had to cleanse himself before joining us."

A rather short, portly man took a seat on one of the many benches in the room. "I hear we've lost two of our men—Sitka and Stau."

"Curse them," another growled.

"Put the blame where it belongs, Setep. The guards obey their king. The fault lies with the cursed son of Aha."

A deep voice interrupted. "That is the truth of it, Setmena. The king is the killer."

Their mumbling of agreement filled the underground chamber.

As leader, Setmena took a seat behind the only table. "The bad news is that we failed to capture the princess and lost our gold. But I have another plan to earn the money we need."

Setep said, "Shouldn't we remain hidden until the excitement of the failed kidnapping is forgotten?"

Setmena frowned. "We could do that, friends, but do we want to bring the throne down or not?"

His band of followers growled in agreement.

"Then hear this. Another of the king's fledglings has flown the nest and is bound for the city of Awen as we speak. The Crown Prince heads for the Military Academy to train as an officer. We have followers in Awen who can help us. Even though it is the city of light, the powers of darkness will easily overpower them." He said it with such conviction his followers pounded their fists on the table.

At that instant, the priest of Set entered the chamber. He wore somber colors of his god. When he removed his head covering, it revealed the large ornate necklace with the image of the god of darkness in the center of it. All other gods and goddesses worshiped by the people of the Black Land were of real animals or persons.

Not Set. He was a god like no other. Resembling the composite of an aardvark, donkey, jackal or fox, he had a curved snout, long rectangular ears, and thin-forked tail on a canine body.

Statues of the god were so horrible they made pregnant women miscarry.

"What can we do to help our friends in Awen, Master?" Setep asked.

Setmena got up from the table and walked to the center of the room. By then, ten other men had joined them.

"I, and four of you, will go to the wicked city of Awen where we will join our brothers. Together, we will take the first step in bringing down the royal house of Aha."

There was more cheering and pounding of fists.

Setmena selected four volunteers. "We will leave for the north in two days. Prepare yourself for what is to come. Can you kill without any thoughts of remorse or regret? Bring your sharpest dagger. The guards will check for weapons at the many control posts along the way. We are good citizens on our way to worship at the temple of Ra." He turned his head and spat on the floor. "Set forgive my blasphemy."

The priest of the temple told them to kneel and he gave an incantation for protection. He used a language thought dead in the city of the old capital. It was, in fact, forbidden.

"Death to the royal family," Setmena shouted as they prepared to leave the chamber.

"Death," the men repeated heading out into the darkness, their black robes flowing like an evil plague about to cover the earth.

4

"What do you mean I will not have my own room? Do you know who I am?"

Ko cringed when the Crown Prince asked that of the Academy Commander.

"Forgive, Highness. We must have three men in a room in the barracks. We have allowed Prince Ako to be in your room, but there will be one other student in there with you."

"The king will hear of this," Jet growled.

The commander's face remained impassive. "Indeed he will, Highness. We are following his orders. In fact, you both must also remove your royal bands and dress like the other trainees."

"Let's go, Ko," Jet said. He turned to leave but the commander shouted at them.

"Stand where you are lowly toads! You will go to your room and prepare for a general assembly when the trumpet sounds."

Ko said, "Can we leave our gold bands with you, Commander? They are worth a considerable sum."

"Of course. They will be put in a treasure storeroom."

Jet removed his thin band and handed it to Ko who in turn gave them to the officer. "Let's go friend," Ko said.

The Crown Prince grumbled but stormed out of the office. "I've never been so insulted, Ko."

The commander followed them. "Wait, Royal Toad. Your father has said you are to shave off your princely braid. It will make you safer here and not a target."

"No, absolutely not," Jet said.

"Please, Cousin. I agree with the king. We need to look like all the other soldiers in training."

The commander clapped his hands and his aide hurried to him. "Bring the barber and a basin of warm water to my office. Be quick about it."

A few minutes later, the aide returned with the man but the Crown Prince would only allow Ko to touch him. It didn't take long, and Ko gave the gold adornment on the end of the braid to the commander for safe keeping.

Ko said, "Now, let's try to find our room."

The royals walked into the courtyard and headed for a bench. Jet's face had darkened and he continued to grumble. Then he blurted out, "I'm taking the next ship home, Ko. I will not stay here."

Ko released a long sigh. "Think, Cousin. You will be disgraced in the eyes of all the men in the army and the Royal Guards. They will think the heir to the throne is incapable of fighting like them. Why then should they follow him?"

"You go too far, Ko. Guard your tongue."

Ko dared to respond. "Think a moment, brother. Here we are all equal. In reality, we are not of course, but we must show the officers we have the ability to lead. Let's agree to be toads, but the best toads in the barracks."

At that moment, another recruit interrupted. He was about the same height as the princes, and his shaved head dripped with sweat. He wore a faded garment and was barefoot. By his hands, it was easy to see he did manual labor. "I'm looking for the Osiris barracks."

Ko shrugged. So are we, I'm afraid."

The young man sat on the grass in the shade. "I am Hepu from a small village near Thinis."

"I am Ko from Memphis and this is Jet."

Jet nodded but didn't say anything.

An officer approached them and shouted, "You lazy sons of toads. Get a move on."

"Where is Osiris, sir?" Ko asked.

The officer growled. "It's the blue building with the green flag, idiots. Now get out of here you miserable troop of baboons."

That made Jet laugh and he couldn't stop as they ran toward the building with a green flag outside. Between breaths he said, "Merry would love hearing him call us baboons."

"What's so funny about baboons?" Hepu asked.

"Have you never seen one?" Ko asked. "There are plenty in the hills around Thinnis."

"No, only a monkey once."

"They're like monkeys, only bigger and angrier," Jet said. "Just like me."

That made Hepu smile and they had but a short distance to reach their building.

When they entered the barracks, they found their room occupied by two other recruits.

Ko said, "I think you men have the wrong room. We have been assigned room three."

One of them put his hands on his hips aggressively. "We were here first you pond scum. Find your own room."

Ko looked at Jet and they moved toward the intruders.

"Leave, you pair of jackals! This is our assigned room," Jet warned.

The shorter of the two men took a swing at Ko but the prince was quick on his feet and dodged the blow. When he swung his right arm, his fist connected with the man's jaw sending him sprawling over the cots. The other tried to grab Jet from behind, but Hepu struck him on the back of the neck knocking him to the floor.

Jet jumped on the first intruder, holding him down.

Rubbing his jaw, the man said, "All right! We're going."

They took their bags from under the beds and left the room.

Jet rubbed his hands together and grinned. "We're not bad for toads, heh?"

"You fight pretty well for city boys," Hepu said.

"City boys? What do you mean?" Ko asked.

"Well, look at your hands—lily white and not a bit of tough skin on them." He walked around them studying first one and then the other. "Tsk, tsk," the farmer mumbled. "It's a wonder you two can fight at all. You can't be very tough."

"What are we some kind of cattle, Hepu?" Ko asked.

Suddenly, the young man stood still and his face changed. "Wait," he said. He moved closer and then backed up before falling prostrate on the floor, the palms of his hands held up to the two other men.

"Forgive me, Highness. I didn't see the small tattoo on the back of the neck. I am so stupid. I really am a toad."

Jet looked at Ko and smiled. "Get up, Hepu and look at my neck. I too have the mark."

"Gods, what will you do to me? Please, young masters. I must become an officer. My family needs the money." He couldn't raise his head to face them. "Mercy, my Lords. Please do not have me killed. The family needs me here."

Ko laughed and collapsed across one of the cots. "We will not do anything to you. His majesty has sent us to the academy to become officers too. We don't want the other trainees to know who we are, so it must be our secret for a while at least."

"But your accent is like mine. You speak no differently," Hepu said.

"That's because we grew up near Thinnis before moving to the capital. Why wouldn't we speak like you?" Jet asked.

Hepu was silent awhile. He put his bag on another of the beds and sat down. "You are both princes then?"

Ko nodded. "Yes, I am the cousin of this lowly toad, and I am the king's nephew."

Jet said, "The gods have selected me to be the Crown Prince. The king is my father."

"Oh no. No, no. . . I can't stay here, my Lords."

"Hepu," Ko said. "If you don't stay, we will have to kill you because you know too much. Understood?"

Hepu look shocked until Jet and Ko began to laugh. He then ran his thumb across his bottom lip. "Sealed," he said. "Thank you great Lords."

A trumpet sounded in the courtyard.

"Assembly," Ko said. "I wonder if we can leave our bags here without fear of thieves getting in."

"We are on the honor system, aren't we? They should be," Hepu said.

Ko said, "Then let's go."

Jet walked behind the two of them. "What are we going to call you, Hepu? Let me see, we can't call you Poo—no, that will never do. It will have to be Hep. Do you agree?"

"Yes, High. . .I mean yes, but everybody at home calls me Digger."

"Why is that?" Ko asked.

"I'm the best farmer in our village. I can dig rows for planting deeper and straighter than anyone else."

"Maybe we can visit your place someday," Jet said.

Because he sounded almost like an ordinary person, Jet's remark made Ko smile.

Over the next few weeks, Jet and Ko did so well and had no trouble making friends. The other recruits liked Digger too. Good natured, he could hold his beer and tell amusing stories about his life on the farm.

One day, when their classes in archery and hand-to-hand combat were over, the commander called an assembly.

"Men, you will go on patrol in two days, to the edge of the western desert. Several caravans have been attacked and the governor has asked us to rid the region of bandits."

A cheer went up from the trainees.

Jet said, "Finally, we're going to see if all this training has done us any good."

Digger scratched his head. "It'll be good to get away from here for a while."

Captain Renni, one of the instructors, said, "Horus brigade will be led by acting sergeant Jet with Dig as his aide. Ra brigade will follow sergeant Ko and Batu. This road is well-travelled and can be dangerous. Choose your best swordsmen. You've all done well in archery, so everyone should take their bows. Spend the time left checking your weapons and arrows. Remember, we'll leave at dawn in two days."

The trainees cheered again and slapped each other on the back.

As the three roommates checked weapons and packs, the commander's aide stopped by their room. "Major Menkhaf is asking for sergeant Ako to report immediately to his office."

Ko saluted, fist to chest, and when the aide had gone, asked, "Why me? I haven't done anything." He walked to the open window. "Could it be bad news from home?"

Jet said, "Stop worrying about it. Go and find out. That's an order."

"You can't order me, Sergeant Toad. But I'm on my way."

Ko knocked on the office door and when told to come in, he entered. He stood at attention studying the officer behind the desk. Major Menkhaf looked different, at least from what he could remember of their first visit to the man's office.

"Ah, Sergeant, come in and sit down."

"Thank you, sir."

Solidly built, the major kept his hair very short. He still had the appearance of a younger man and everyone at the academy respected him for it. They had seen him in mock battles, defeating even the strongest of the trainees.

"Highness, I called you in to make a report. I've spoken to your instructors but now I want to hear from you. How are you fitting in to this program? More particularly, how is the Crown Prince doing? I hear only good things about him."

Ko relaxed. "He's a completely different person, Major. He wanted to go home the first day, but so did a lot of us. I think his not having to live up to what people expect of him made him relax and be himself. He's going to be a fine soldier. He's a good fighter, excellent in archery and I can't beat him in hand-to-hand."

"Ah, thank the gods, I was certain that pride of his would keep him from his true potential. I am glad to hear he has adjusted well. What about you, Highness?"

Ko relaxed even more. "I like it here, sir. I've always wanted to try to be as good a soldier as my father is, and I'm getting there. I've even beaten Jet at archery."

"Good. We all respect Lord Akhom. King Aha honored him when he made him his blood brother. I have no doubt you will follow in his footsteps." The major cleared his throat, paused and asked, "And do your comrades know who you are?"

"No one has said anything, Major, but I'm sure they have seen our royal tattoos."

"Of course, I'd forgotten about them. I'm going to announce to everyone who you are."

"Please do not do that, Major. Let our comrades tell us when they're ready. Right now, we're all good friends—well, everyone but Pentu because we kicked him out of our room when we first arrived, but even he will come around."

"What about Digger? Has he told anyone?"

"No. He would never tell, on my honor."

"He and the crown prince could be brothers. Have you noticed?"

"I agree. There is a strong resemblance. It is uncanny."

"We wish you a good hunting for those bandits. Horus go with you."

"Thank you, Major." Ko saluted, did an about face, and left the office.

Back in the barracks, Jet wanted to know if he was in trouble.

"There was no trouble, Cousin. The major is pleased with us because he's only heard good things from our instructors about how we've adjusted to life at the garrison."

"Really?"

Digger laughed. "Well, you've certainly poured beeswax over their eyes."

Ko said, "I am looking forward to tonight. The older students are presenting a play about how King Narmer united the Black Lands. Captain Renni said several young women from Awen will be hostesses and serve refreshments."

"Women? Now there's something to be excited about," Jet said.

"Are you going, Dig?" Ko asked.

The young farmer lay stretched out on his bed. "No, I'm still sore from my last combat exercise. My stomach's a little queasy."

"Very well. We will kiss the girls for you."

Digger threw one of his sandals at them as they hurried out of the room.

They walked across the lawn and through the garden in front of the Academy. Jet said, Do you really think Dig's coming down with something? Maybe he's just shy with girls."

Ko shook his head. "Let him rest. He did take quite a beating in our last hand-to-hand."

After the theatre presentation, the princes spent time vying for the attention of the most beautiful hostesses. One of the trainees brought out his three-stringed harp and sang love songs, making the young women clap their hands. Major Menkhaf was present and he nodded his approval when asked if the young people could dance.

Many beers later, Ko and Jet reluctantly left the common room and helped steady each other as they headed across the garden. Reaching the barracks, they used the walls for support until finally reaching their room.

"The door's ajar," Ko said.

"Dig must have gone out and forgotten to shut it."

They pushed the door open and walked in. Ako used the small flint and lit the oil lantern near his cot.

The light revealed Digger lying face down asleep.

"I just want to sleep for a month," Jet sighed, collapsing on his cot.

Ko accidently bumped Dig's bed hard enough where it should have awakened him. "Sorry, Dig."

When his friend didn't respond, Ko said, "I think Dig is really out, he didn't move when I bumped him."

"Let him be. Sleeping off, whatever he's got, will do him good."

Ko wasn't sure. He touched Dig's arm and it felt really cold. "Something is wrong."

Jet got up, and brought the lamp closer to Dig's cot. "Turn him over."

Ko rolled their friend over and both men cried out in horror. Dig's face was black and his swollen tongue was sticking out.

"Gods!" Jet exclaimed, almost dropping the lamp.

A rope tied around their friend's neck had cut off all circulation, and in the darkness looked like a snake.

They stepped back and sat on Ko's cot. "Who would do such a thing?" he asked.

"He's only a farmer who wanted to be a soldier," Jet said. "It doesn't make sense."

Ko finally got up enough courage to approach Dig's cot again. He gritted his teeth as he loosened the rope and threw it on the floor.

"What's this," he said, picking up a small piece of papyrus lying by the body. He opened it and whispered, "There's a message, Jet."

His cousin came over and together they read:

The crown prince is dead.
Set is victorious.

5

The common room of the barracks soon filled with loud conversation about Digger's murder. None of the trainees wanted to sit and be quiet, but when Major Menkhaf entered, they took their places.

The commander led Jet and Ko into the hall and they stood on either side of him.

"Quiet, men. Give me your attention," the major said.

When the noise stopped, he cleared his throat. "These two members of our garrison you know well, but you don't know everything about them. Jet's actual name is Crown Prince Djet, son of King Djed, Blessed Son of Horus."

At those words, everyone in the hall except Ko and the Major fell prostrate, palms extended toward the prince.

Jet said, "Please take your places, friends." He was suddenly embarrassed.

The trainees stood and took their seats again.

The major said, "His roommate we know as Ko, but he is Prince Ako, son of Prince Akhom, brother of his majesty."

The trainees applauded, and Ko smiled.

Menkhaf continued. "As you know, their friend, Digger, was murdered last night, strangled by a rope in his bed. The assassin mistook him for Prince Jet and left a message declaring he had killed the heir to the throne."

A buzz in the hall grew as the young men began to understand what happened.

One of them shouted, "Who would want to do such a cowardly thing, Major?"

Ko reached out and touched the major's arm. "May I respond, sir?"

The major nodded.

Ko spoke in a loud voice. "We know who has done this evil deed. There is no question. It began years ago when the sons of Set murdered our beloved King Aha."

As one voice, the young warriors chanted, "We honor his name."

Ko continued. "As the major said, my father and the king were brothers. He was able to kill the assassin, disbanding those who worship Set, or so we thought. Recently they have reappeared. With this attempt on the Crown Prince's life, they mean to bring down the king and his family."

Murmurs of protest spread and Ko paused a moment.

"Kill them all," someone shouted.

"Death to the followers of Set," others cried.

The major raised his hand. "Prince Djet would like to say something else."

Jet raised his hand, palm toward them as if taking a vow and spoke in a loud clear voice. "You men know me as Jet, not his highness, and I want that to continue. You have made both of us feel a part of this garrison and we are grateful. We will always know each other on a first name basis—at least in private."

His friends laughed and clapped louder.

A friend shouted, "We knew all along who you were, Jet. It is hard not to notice the way you speak, and in the bath, the royal tattoos gave you away."

Jet laughed. "You are right, Babu, and thank you for treating us as one of you. Please do not change.

You've made us feel like regular trainees instead of pampered royals."

Once again, their comrades stomped their feet and shouted his name. The prince looked at his cousin with a big grin.

"Major," one of the men called out.

"What is it?"

"Why can't we go out and try to find these motherless sons of Set?"

The major encouraged the two royals to return to their brigades and take their places.

Another asked, "Will we have to be put to death now if we dare touch these royal people?"

Everyone laughed.

Jet said, "If we did, anyone who fought me in hand-to-hand will die—and that is everyone in this room."

His comrades shouted him down, laughing and patting him on the back. Jet shouted, "Majesty— throw them to the crocodiles!"

The trainees roared even louder.

Major Menkhaf stood silent while their genuine camaraderie played out. When they settled down again, he stepped forward. "Instead of our campaign against the thieves that would have started in the morning, we will leave here by groups of four. Sergeants from the local garrison will lead each group. You are to seek out these serpents of Set and arrest them. Take them to the stockade for questioning. Arm yourselves with your daggers and be prepared for attacks. Look out for each other. And remember, the killers don't know the prince is still alive

The trainees stomped their feet with approval.

Someone shouted, "Jet and Ko can't go with us, Major. They're already targets."

"No, Major," Ko shouted. "We can't have our friends put their lives in danger and we not do anything. The gods would not approve."

"Enough," the major said raising his hand for silence. "As long as the king has placed you here, you are mine to command. Those are his orders. You will obey us, or return to Memphis."

Jet said, "To hear is to obey, major."

"Dismissed," Menkhaf ordered.

"But Major. . ."Ko started.

"Follow me, Highness," the officer ordered.

The two princes followed him outside into the garden. "I had to be sure no one could overhear." He led them to a bench and they sat down. "There has already been an arrest this morning. One of the guards stopped a drunken man in town. He must have been celebrating the death of who he thought was the crown prince, but passed out in the street. When the guard found him, he turned him over to tie his hands and saw the forbidden mark of Set on his neck behind the ear."

"Gods!" Ko said. "Thank Horus for that guard."

"Indeed," the major said. "When asked his name, he was proud of it and gave it willingly. His name is Setep and his accent is similar to you toads. That means he comes from around Thinis."

Jet said, "But how did he know I would be here? There must be a Setite at the palace."

Ko shook his head. "Not necessarily. It was no secret that we were coming to Awen for training. A messenger pigeon could have been sent even before we sailed."

Jet said, "I will personally strangle the man you arrested until his face turns black. I will never forget the horrible look on Digger's face. "Please gods, let me do this." His emotions affected his voice and he couldn't go on.

They were silent a moment, and then Jet said, "I will see that our friend receives the best embalming at the House of the Dead, Major. Will you see that his remains are removed?"

"Yes, Highness. His family will be honored." He paused for a moment and then added, "I will see that our comrade receives the best embalming at the House of the Dead." The major added, we didn't want to tell everyone about the arrest. We need to find out how many followers of Set might be in Awen."

Ko asked, "Will you let us help interrogate the prisoner?"

Menkhaf nodded. "I do insist that two guards be with you at all times."

"Agreed," Jet said.

That afternoon as they washed up behind the barracks, Ko said, "I have an idea."

Jet toweled off and took a seat on one of the wooden benches. "All right. What is it?"

"We should play up how much Digger looked like you, Cousin. The resemblance was so close he was mistaken for you. Let's wait until the middle of the night. We'll ask the major for the kilt and belt Digs was wearing. You can put some flour on your face to whiten it, and then appear as if Digger's ghost is in the cell. Maybe it will scare the truth out of him."

Jet frowned. "You can't be serious." He paused and then said, "Everyone is afraid of spirits and ghosts—so it might work. The prisoner has never heard me speak so that won't be a problem. I'll have a dagger on me in case he attacks Digger's ghost as well." In his excitement, Jet stood up abruptly forgetting his towel. "It might work. That is a genius of an idea, Cousin."

"Cover yourself, Great Bull of Horus! Let's go inside and work out the details. We'll have to convince the local guards on duty of what we are doing."

For the rest of the day, they talked about their plans. Barrack-mates helped them find some of the objects they needed. One went to the temple of Horus to borrow things from the priests. Another went to the local stockade to inform them that two of the major's men would be coming in the middle of the night to interrogate the prisoner.

That night, when it was time to go, Ko used flour and water to paint Jet's face, torso, arms and legs with white flour. He placed the thin gold crown on his cousin's head, and then put on what he was going wear. They walked the to the city stockade and did not encounter anyone. When the guards on duty saw Jet, they jumped from fright and had to be reassured who he was.

"Quiet," Jet whispered. "Where are the musicians?"

"We're here," a man replied holding a lute. Two others carried flutes and sistrums.

"Good," Ko said. "We want ethereal music—something sounding like what the music in our second life might be like. It must bring fear into that cell."

"I'll send the signal for you to start playing," Ko added.

The musicians nodded and went to prepare outside the window of the stockade.

"Are we ready, Cousin? Ko asked. "This is all on you, now. Horus give you strength."

Setep, the prisoner, lay on the floor of the cell and knew he was going to die. He was just glad he had accomplished his mission. The crown prince was dead and Cobra, the leader of the sons of Set, killed by Aha's family, had been avenged by what he did last night.

He drank a little more water from a clay jug. He thought it tasted sour, but gulped it down anyway. The moon had risen and its bright tendrils reached through the small window of his cell. As he stared at the light, he felt his head begin to spin. He shifted on the floor and closed his eyes.

Strange music filtered through the window sounding like it was not of this world—it was eerie and mysterious and made Setep's skin crawl.

A tongue of thin blue smoke crept in under the door, filling the cell with its jasmine fragrance. Suddenly, with a flash of light the cell door burst open. .

Setep squinted and a chill ran down the center of his spine. Someone or something was standing in the doorway.

"Release me, Setep," its voice cried out to him.

The prisoner jumped up and backed away until pressed against the far wall.

"Setep, it is I, Prince Djet, son of the king. You must set me free."

More smoke and music filled his small cell.

The voice said, "My Ka is a prisoner here and cannot move to the second life. It is you who hold me here."

Setep's head continued to spin. "No, no, go away."

The mysterious figure moved inside and drew closer to him. He couldn't believe what he was seeing.

It was Prince Djet, and he cried out. "Go away. I killed you—now go with the dead."

The ghost-like apparition moved closer. "The leader of Set's followers is ashamed of you. You killed me dishonorable—with a rope, and not the clean sword. You disobeyed him."

"No, no," Setep cried. "Setau wouldn't say that. None of the followers of Great Set would say it. They know I serve the temple. All Thinis knows of our loyalty to our god." He couldn't stop whimpering and held his head between his hands.

A loud thud made the prisoner cover his ears. When he looked up again, a second figure stood next to the ghost. Setep screamed. It was a human creature with the great head of the falcon god, Horus. Its black eyes sent fear into his heart.

"Set is defeated, Setep," Horus said. "I am ruler of this land. Your Ka will die and never enter the second life." The great god reached out and touched the ghost of the crown prince who handed him a silver sword. "Give me the names of your brotherhood."

Setep wanted to back away, but was unable to move.

One of the guards entered and stood behind the two strange beings. He held a narrow piece of charcoal to write on a thin piece of papyrus.

The god moved closer and Setep fell on his face before it. He blurted out the names and the guard wrote them down.

The "dead" prince held the sword toward the prisoner and Setep screamed in pain as the sword was plunged into his chest, piercing his heart. He collapsed and everything went black as he closed his eyes.

"Die, dog," Jet exclaimed as he pulled Akhom's sword out of the assassin.

"Well done, Cousin." We now have the name of the leader in Thinis and those using the ruin of the old temple of the evil god—forbidden by the crown."

Guards entered the cell and took out the body.

"Throw him to the crocodiles, men," Jet said. "His Ka is no more."

"Major Menkhaf told us to do whatever you command, my Lord. We will obey."

"Very good. We are returning to the garrison," Jet said.

Ko gave the musicians silver coins and thanked them.

On the walk back to the barracks, they met an elderly man in the street who fell over in a faint when he saw the ghost and the giant figure of Horus coming toward him.

Ko removed the large head of Horus, bent over and felt the old man's pulse. "He's all right, just passed out." He couldn't help laughing. "I don't know what I would think either if I saw us coming down the street."

Jet chuckled as they neared their barracks. Behind their room, he washed off the flour paste, making him scratch all over once more.

Their friends met them and took the head of Horus, makeup, and incense back to the temple.

Exhausted from their theatrics, the two cousins collapsed on their beds and fell asleep.

The last thing Ko saw in his mind's eye was the expression on the face of the prisoner when the god Horus walked into the cell. As he drifted off, the slight curve of a smile touched his lips.

During the morning meal, Jet asked Ko, "Where did this idea of the ghost come from?"

Ko smiled and put down his bread covered with fresh honey. "It was a long time ago, when I had only seen ten summers. I went to a trial with my father and the high priest of Amun was charged by King Aha to find the murderer of a priest. The killer was supposedly a soldier in father's regiment.

"They had arrested four suspects, and the high priest was unable to decide who was guilty. It had grown dark outside and imagine our horror when we saw the ghost of the dead priest enter, his finger pointing toward the four men. The troubled spirit glowed in an unearthly light and in a deep haunting voice shouted, 'There he is.' When it drew closer, the guilty soldier fell face down, trembling with fear. The other three soldiers quickly moved away."

"Afterward, father took me behind the temple where the high priest, a good friend of father's, showed us how it was done. We even saw where the priests had hollowed out some of the great statues of the gods. By speaking through a small opening, they were able to speak to the people in mysterious voices as if the gods were present in the temple. It was a great disappointment to me. I still remember how sad I felt that some of the religious magic I believed as a child was not real.

"Priests," Jet grumbled. "I don't trust priests. Never have."

For a moment, Ko thought he saw someone moving in the shadows of the bushes outside. He stood and hurried to the window, but when he stuck his head out, didn't see anyone. Shrugging, he went back to his place at the table and finished his bread.

6

Queen Nakhneith and her daughter sat in the front room of the king's palace. Built of polished limestone, the walls were inlaid with beautiful images of the royal family—kings Narmer and Aha and, most recently, their descendant Djed.

Light yellow thin linen curtains danced in the breezes from the sacred river. They sat on comfortable blue cushions covering two divans. Her majesty embroidered a scene of brown and white waterfowl flying up from the water.

"You miss him, don't you?" Merry's mother asked.

"Who?"

"Why Ako, young lady? You do know he's seen sixteen summers and you only fourteen?"

"Of course, Mother. It's true, I do miss him."

At that moment their steward interrupted. "Majesty."

"Yes, what is it?"

"There's a young man here who insists on seeing Princess Mereneith."

"He insists? Only a royal can insist in this palace."

"He will not go away, Majesty. I even threatened to have the guards remove him, but he won't leave."

"Very well, bring in two guards with you and show him in. You may stay with us, Intef."

"Yes, Great Lady." The steward left and returned with the guards and a poorly dressed young man not much older that the princess. He bowed to the floor before the queen."

"Who are you and how dare you insist on seeing us." The queen said.

The young man stood without permission and bowed his head to her. "I have a present for the princess, Majesty."

"Oh, for me?" Merry said, her curiosity drawing her closer to the stranger.

"Will you accept it, Beautiful One?" he asked.

"Where is it? Show it to me."

"I'll bring it in. Wait here, Princess," the young man said.

The queen interrupted. "You will do no such thing. Guard, go with this impertinent intruder. Examine the gift and if it is safe, return with him."

The young man returned a few moments with the guard and carrying a small cage made from woven water reeds. A green linen cloth covered it. He pulled off the cloth and Merry looked inside.

"It's alive," she exclaimed. "What is it?" She moved closer and shouted, "It's a kitten." She clapped her hands with delight. Thank you, Bastet."

Queen Nakhtneith stood and approached the cage. "A kitten? Who would send a kitten as a gift to a princess?"

The young man bowed again. "He said he was a prince, Majesty, and that his name was Ako."

Merry laughed happily and spun around in a circle. "How wonderful."

The young man continued. "He also said, Princess, that since he wasn't around to protect you, he sent you this descendant of Bastet whose head is that of a lioness. She will protect you because she is a princess like you."

Merry opened the lid of the small cage and lifted out the mewling kitten. She held her close to her bosom. "Oh, she's purring."

She held her up and showed her mother. "What shall I name her?"

The queen smiled and pet the little creature. "Only you can name her, Merry. It is said that a cat will be loyal forever to the one who names it."

The princess turned toward Intef. "Give the young man a gold coin for his service."

"Yes, Highness," Intef replied, motioning for the young man to follow him out with the guards.

"Young man," Merry called the lad back. "You will come back and show me the coin. With a wink in her eye she added, "Do you understand?"

He grinned. "Yes, Highness. I'll be right back."

Merry smiled. She knew that servants were often tempted to withhold small amounts of coin.

Her mother said, "You are learning not to trust everyone, Merry. That is good."

Intef and the guard returned with the young man. He held up the coin to show the princess and bit down on it. "It's good, Highness."

"How are you called?" Merry asked.

"I am called the happiest man in the land for having met you, Highness. But, Beautiful One, my friends call me

"I am called the happiest man in the land for having met you, Highness. But, Beautiful One, my friends call me Maya." Before she could say anything else, he turned, and left the chamber.

Merry laughed, "I like him." She picked up the small cage and walked to her bedchamber. Putting it down, she lay across her bed with the kitten nestled in the bend of her arm.

"I will pray to the cat goddess to name you, little lion."

"Miu," the tiny feline replied. Then she yawned, closed her yellowish green eyes and fell asleep.

In the northern city of Awen, the trainees of the military garrison returned to their barracks. They brought six followers of Set under arrest and locked them up in the guardhouse for interrogation and eventual execution.

In the main hall which was their dining room for the moment, Ko finished his meal and as he passed the officer's table, Major Menkhaf motioned for him to sit down.

"Ko, I want your thoughts on something."

The prince nodded.

"If there is a temple of Set in Thinis, we need to go and arrest this Setau and as many of their followers as we can find."

"I agree, Major."

"I'm sending Captain Renni with a brigade of twenty-five regular guards from the local garrison. I want to send ten of our trainees as well. I would also like you to go. Jet cannot go with you, unfortunately, it is too dangerous for the heir to the throne."

"I understand—but Jet will not. He will be devastated if he cannot go."

"I know, but I'm sending him on another mission. He'll be going with the Army of the North under General Merseruka."

"He'll do well, sir, you know that."

"The general will arrive soon, bringing his warriors. He'll be heading out into the Desert of the Mountain. The king is moving into that region to protect our northern borders."

Ko scratched his head. The 'Desert of the Mountain?' he repeated.

"Yes, it is in the lands east of the Great Sea. The 'Mountain' in question is rumored to be the home of the desert gods." He took a yellow apple from the bowl on the table and bit into it.

"When will we sail for Thinis?" Ko asked.

"In the morning. I'd love to come with you but I've been ordered to stay with the general," the major said.

"That's a shame, sir. We still have much to learn from you."

Major Menkhaf stood. "Enough of your attempts at flattery lowly toad."

Ko laughed and headed out of the hall.

The mighty galley, Breath of Horus sailed south against the river's mighty current.

Ko stood in the bow, reveling in the cool wind blowing through his thick hair. The fragrances of the river were the best perfume in the Black Land. There were lotus blossoms, and deep bluish purple water hyacinths. The thick and lush riverbanks on each side resembled the long green arms of the gods welcoming him home.

"What are you thinking, Ko?" Captain Renni asked.

"Family, sir. I was thinking about how much I missed them." He grinned. Don't tell them I ever said that, Captain."

"I understand. One must not show any weakness. Is that it?"

"Yes, Captain. One of the rules we've learned for being a good solider and leader."

"Well said." Renni leaned against the railing. Older by ten summers, the captain leaned against the railing. He and Ko were about the same height. He had a straight nose and strong chin. His large eyes never stopped moving. Straight teeth and added to the brilliance of his smile. He was also well-muscled, and his bare chest bore a light dusting of brown hair. "As for me," he began, "I can only think of Nofret, my intended. She's beautiful and we were going to marry last year before the inundation of the river. But her father died, and they needed her back home."

"I'm sorry sir. Where is home?"

"Meydum, not far from here."

"We could stop there for a short visit, Captain."

Renni shook his head. "Not now, soldiers. Remember, we are on a mission."

"Tell me about her sir, if you care to."

Renni put his foot up on the lowest bar of the railing and stared out across the river as if he could see her. "She's more beautiful than the images we see of the goddess Isis. She is perfect in every way, body, mind and her inner Ka. We feel as if we are one."

Ko simply murmured, "um hum."

"What about your girl, Ko?"

"I don't have a girl, Captain. Oh, don't get me wrong, there are plenty of young women at court. Father would like me to marry, but I haven't found the one for me. I'll know when I meet her."

"Then I wish you the best, Prince. I understand that royals cannot always marry the ones they love, so I'll pray the gods help you find the right one."

As they passed near the riverbank on one of the many curves, children jumped up and down trying to get their attention. They laughed and shouted until Ko and Renni waved to them.

"Did anyone know that there was a forbidden temple of Set in the city of Thinis?" Renni asked.

"You know, Captain, don't you think this Setau and the other followers will know we are coming and will have fled the city?"

"Probably, but they must have families in Thinis if that's where they've been living. Maybe we can use them to flush out the leaders."

The intense heat diminished late in the afternoon and the ship prepared to anchor mid-stream for the night. The guards from Awen enjoyed the company of the younger trainees. That evening they shared fresh bread and broiled fish prepared by the ship's crew. Many of the men had been fishing over the sides all day. They also bought fresh bread from a small village on the way and dozens of jars of beer which they hung over the side in the water to keep cool.

The docked at Thinnis in the afternoon of the second day. The officer in charge of the local garrison met them. Captain Renni's trainees followed the officer to the city garrison for the night. They were crowded, but everyone eventually found a place to unroll his blanket.

As Ko drifted off to sleep, his head filled with what might happen in the morning when they began their search for the Setites.

Up north, in Awen, Prince Jet was disappointed he could not sail to Thinis. He stood at the dock as General Merseruka's ship arrived. Soldiers on board shouted and cheered as their officer stepped off the ship.

Major Menkhaf and the prince met him and the general knelt on one knee in front of the Crown Prince and saluted. "Greetings son of Djed, King of the Two Lands."

Jet walked toward him and bowed his head slightly. "Welcome General of the Army. We are yours to command."

Merseruka stood and smiled. "Well, that is something you do not hear often from a royal, Highness."

The shipload of warriors cheered again, slapping their shields with their swords.

The major moved forward and saluted the general. "Come, and refresh yourself, General."

"Lead on. I'm glad to be on land again."

Jet followed the officers through the rows of local soldiers and trainees standing at attention. Three horses awaited them at the top of the road leading to the river. The general mounted a magnificent stallion as did Jet and the major. When they reached the garrison and dismounted, trainees took their reins and led the horses to the stables.

A trainee brought Merseruka a basin of water and linen towel to wash his face and hands.

In Major Menkhaf's small apartment, the general chose to sit in the only large, comfortable chair. "Ah, that's better."

Jet sat near him. "I hear the armies of the Asiatics in the north have thousands of horses, General. I wish there were more in Kemet." He thought it amusing that his people referred to everyone north of Kemet as Asiatics.

The major said, "I have heard in battle their horses pull their soldiers on wheeled platforms which allow their archers to fire at the enemy."

Jet said, "It sounds dangerous."

The general nodded. "Yes, it is of course, but they have a great advantage. We must raise great numbers of horses. I know this will bring us success in battle."

Menkhaf summoned his aide who then served the mid-day meal. Several trainees helped serve broiled fish, greens, fresh bread and slices of sweet yellow melon. They left two large jars of beer and cups on the table.

As they ate, they shared stories about their families and old campaigns. Jet ate silently, nodding and smiling now and then.

Afterward, the three men moved to the shade of palms near the barracks.

Jet asked the general, "Tell me about why we are beginning a campaign in the desert, General. That is, if you can."

The veteran officer loosened his belt and patted his belly before answering. "Our scouts have told us for several weeks that the Asiatics have moved south into the desert of the mountain."

"Which mountain?" the major asked. "What it is called?"

"I am told there is a very large mountain on which the gods live. The region is also home to the gods of the winds."

"Gods of the wind," Jet repeated. "You mean like our Shu, our god of the wind?"

The general shrugged. "I don't know if our gods live in other lands or in the desert. Perhaps we will find out. Don't spread this to my men. Soldiers are superstitious enough without adding the fear of other gods."

Jet rubbed his shaved head. He missed his princely braid. "What a thought, my Lord General. Does Horus go with us when we go to other lands? I pray he does, but I have never thought about it before."

The major said, "I wouldn't ask it of our priests, you know how parochial they are. We certainly won't share anything with your men, General."

Merseruka leaned forward and addressed the prince. "Now, Highness, we are pleased to have you on our march. We always feel the gods take better care of the army when a son of the royal family is with us, or when he wills it, even the king himself."

Jet grinned. "I am honored, my Lord to be a bringer of good fortune."

The older man chuckled, and then abruptly his face changed to show concern. "I did not mean to offend, Highness. We know you bring your fighting skills which the major assures me are excellent."

"No offense taken, General. I would pray that Horus will come with us and will help us defeat the Asiatic invaders."

Major Menkhaf asked, "How many ships are coming, General?"

"In this first wave, there are thirty ships in total with two-hundred men each. It will take about a week to get them ready to march. Then, another wave of ships a week later will bring us to twelve thousand."

"As many as that," Menkhaf said. "Feeding so many will be an enormous task."

"The quartermasters are loading sacks of beans and flour for bread. My biggest concern is water. Wagons will pull barrels with us after filling them here at the river. We have horses, but not enough. Your father, Highness, has doubled the number, purchasing them from Jedda, across the Eastern Sea. They have begun breeding them in the delta where we have plenty of grass for them."

"What about their strange military wagons?" Jet asked.

"They call them chariots, Highness. We must adapt them to our land. Theirs are too heavy and do not travel over rocks very well. But we do have a few at the moment. Some of our best riders have trained with archers on board. It is a frightening thing to see the speed at which an arrow can pierce a man's chest—splitting it open."

Jet swallowed hard and tried to put it out of his mind.

7

Captain Bakaa and his men followed on foot a poorly maintained road outside the city of Thinis.

Ko asked, "Are you sure this is the way?"

"Yes, several of our unit saw what they thought was a hidden entrance under an abandoned temple of Hapi up ahead."

When they reached it, one of the men shouted, "Here it is, Ko. It's under this fallen column."

The small temple had once been beautiful. Colors on the painted decorations were still evident, and various carved images of river creatures lay tossed about. Dozens of columns reclined on each other, as if toppled by an earthquake.

The prince, now a temporary sergeant, bent down and looked into the dark entrance beneath the column.

"Good. Let's send two men down and see what's there," Bakaa said.

Babu said, "I'll go."

"And I'll go with him," Khenti said.

The two men squeezed under the column and into the passage below. "We'll need a torch, Captain," Babu called up to him.

"I brought a flint with me," Ko said. "Find a dried palm branch."

They wound dried fiber around the end of the frond, Ko struck the flint with his dagger causing a spark to ignite it, then, he passed the torch down to the two men.

Ko stood on the fractured steps leading into the sacred place, looking at the remnants of what had been the roof lying on the floor. The image of Hapi was still in place—a beautifully sculpted image of the river god whose name gave the river its name—'giver of life.'

Stray cats ran out of the building, and their strong smell clung to the ruin.

"I wonder why this temple was abandoned," one of the men said.

Ko asked, "And why would these motherless sons of Set use such a ruin for their meetings?"

"Maybe it's because they felt safe here, Sergeant," Bakaa said. He suddenly became anxious for his men below and hurried back to the underground steps.

They squeezed easily under the broken column but the two men weren't there. A light flickered ahead, and they headed toward it. When they had gone perhaps twenty paces, they found the torch laying on the ground next to two dark shapes.

"It's them," Ko shouted.

Bakaa picked up the torch so they could get a better look. The two trainees lay covered in blood. "Are they. . . ?"

"Yes," Ko replied, straightening up. "Multiple stab wounds to the back. They didn't stand a chance. He moved the torch to light up the surrounding floor. There are also footprints here of several persons."

"Gods," Bakaa swore. "Hurry to the end of the passage. They may still be there. Swords at the ready."

Using the torch to guide them, they discovered an opening at the end of the passage, but there was no one in sight.

Sabu kicked something with his foot. "Look, Sergeant."

Ko walked over and picked up a copper cup. He turned it around and discovered the mark of Set. He headed for the opening and examined it in the sunlight.

Captain Bakaa knelt beside Babu's body. "Well, we've found where they've been meeting. I'm sure they won't come here again. By this foul attack they've shown us they love darkness more than life itself."

"Sabu, hire a donkey and cart," Ko ordered. "We'll take our fallen comrades back to the barracks. I will wait here without men. We can ask the soldiers of the local garrison what to do, and my family will pay for their embalming at the House of the Dead. Their Ka will continue in the second life as heroes in his majesty's service."

"We will remember their names," his men shouted loud enough to frighten the birds from the trees.

"Pentu, leave us and report what we've found. Hurry," Ko said.

"Wait," Bakaa interrupted. "Tell the officer to send a messenger pigeon and warn the guards at the palace to be extra vigilant. Now hurry."

Pentu saluted, and ran off toward town.

Ko and Captain Bakaa sat on a fallen stone column and waited.

"Seth's entrails," Bakaa cursed. "Two casualties and we've only just begun."

Ko regretted the loss of two of his comrades but didn't know how to respond.

"Oh, I'm not blaming you, Sergeant. We should have brought more men to this desolate shrine. It is my responsibility and I will take the blame."

"We will never find the families of these Setites now, Captain."

"Probably not. I'm certain they've left town as well, knowing what their brothers have done."

"Thank you for thinking of sending my family the message, Captain. I didn't even think of them. I'm really not a good soldier or son."

"Enough of such talk, young toad. The priests of Horus teach us that such worrying only brings defeat."

They were silent a while until Ko asked, "What about their remains? Can the local garrison take care of them?"

"Yes, of course. Their families will find honor in the fact that it is the king's nephew who is caring for them. It is a kind thing, Highness."

Ko was embarrassed and didn't respond.

Bakaa studied the copper cup and the imprint of Set's mark pressed into the soft metal. He stood and paced around a bit. "I suggest we begin here—that is, in the neighborhood closest to the ruin. Someone must have seen these men coming and going— perhaps in the middle of the night. They would have had to carry lanterns or torches. Choose men who get along well with people. We don't want any military bullying, understand?"

"Yes, Captain."

A braying donkey signaled Sabu's return with the cart. He brought two linen sheets and they carefully wrapped Babu and Khenti's bodies with them before lifting them into the cart. Bakaa led his men as they walked behind the cart as Sabu drove the donkey along the old back road into the city.

Psar, the officer on duty at the garrison gate, appeared uneasy when first introduced to Prince Ako. He acted flustered and didn't know how to speak in front of the royal. However, when he learned what had happened and saw the bodies in the wagon, he grew angry.

"Two dead on my watch! How is it possible? What addled idiot is responsible, Bakaa?"

"I am," Ko replied.

"Not so, Psar," Bakaa corrected. "I am responsible. I should have had more men with me, but it is my mistake, no one else's."

Psar said in a loud voice, "What do I call you? Highness or Sergeant?"

"I am Sergeant," Ko answered.

Psar's voice was louder still. "Then, Sergeant, you are on report and will spend the next day sharpening and cleaning all of our weapons. Is that clear?"

"Yes, Captain," Ko said, saluting.

"No, he will not, Psar. He is my sergeant, not yours. If there is any discipline to give, I will give it, not you. It is true we are here to help you in the search for these sons of whores, but we do not answer to you." Bakaa, who was a little taller than Psar put his fists on his hips and stared him down.

"Bah. Just keep this palace puff out of my sight. I don't want him anywhere near my men, is that clear?"

"Loud and clear, Psar," Bakaa replied in an even louder voice. "Let's go, Sergeant. The smell in here is beginning to get to me." He pushed past the captain, knocking him out of the way.

Ko saw the look on Psar's face and hurried after his officer. When he caught up with Bakaa, he asked, "Do you two know each other?"

"We were trainees here in Thinis at the same time. He's not a threat."

"Won't we need his help in catching these assassins? Is it wise to antagonize him? I didn't mind doing that detail. I've done it for you many times."

"That isn't the point, Ko. He was showing you no respect, not as a soldier nor as a prince of the house of Djed. I won't permit it." He stopped and turned to face him. "Let's get some food into us, after first making sure we've sent a message to the palace in Memphis. Then we will regroup and make a plan. I still think going door to door in the neighborhood around that desolate shrine is the place to start."

The next day, the prince and captain stood in front of a simple clay-brick house and waited for someone to answer the door. They'd left the garrison early and chose the row of houses closest to the ruined shrine. Door was too kind a description for the tattered cloth hung by a string over the entrance.

"Iwy em hotep," Bakaa called again. "Hello, is anyone here?"

A large full-bodied woman with no teeth moved the curtain aside. A naked child rode on her hip. "What is it?"

Ko said, "We would like to know about the old shrine up the road."

"What about it?"

The child began to cry and the woman called for an older child to take it away.

Ko asked, "Have there been people going to the shrine at night? With torches and things?"

"What is it worth to you?" she said, her lips forming a smile.

The prince took out a copper coin from the pouch inside the waistband of his kilt.

When she saw it, her eyes lit up and she ran her hand through her hair to straighten it. She reached out her hand, but Ko didn't move.

"Tell us what you know, first. Then the coin."

She motioned for him to come closer and it was all Ko could do to keep from becoming ill. The stench of the unwashed peasant overwhelmed him. When he looked down, he discovered the woman was also missing two toes.

She said, "I've seen two men dressed in black, passing by in the middle of the night. I know because my baby was crying and I had to get up. I did hear two of them talking one night and I heard the one call the other Jackal. I thought it strange to be calling a man a jackal." She laughed revealing her gums. "Wives often call their husband's that, but this was different."

Walking outside, she sat on an old wooden bench in front of the house. "Another night I was sitting right here, rocking my daughter back to sleep. A group of men hurried past all dressed in black with hoods covering their heads." She paused and looked at the two men.

"Go on," Bakaa said.

"It was frightening. One of them carried a small child over his shoulder. The child didn't move so I thought it was asleep."

"A child? Are you sure?" Ko asked.

"Yes, but they didn't have it with them when they passed here on the way back to town."

The hair on the back of Ko's neck stood up, and he looked at the captain.

The woman stood, brushed off her tattered robe and was about to enter the house when she stopped and turned back. "We found a small head several days later in the ruin, on the old altar. There were blood stains everywhere."

"Is this true, dear lady?" Ko asked. "You're not making this up for the coin?"

The woman turned toward the house, "Tchay!" she shouted in a loud voice. "Come here husband."

A small man, barely dressed had trouble keeping his tunic on. "What?" he grumbled.

She walked over to him and pushed her finger into his hairy chest. "Wake up and tell these men what we found in the old temple."

The man repeated what the woman, told them. "We don't let the children play there anymore. It is cursed."

"The gods are not pleased, that is certain," Ko said. "We are here to find these men. Their evil deeds must be stopped." He reached into his money pouch and handed the woman five copper coins. It was enough to buy food for a month. "Their evil deeds anger the gods."

Her mouth dropped open and then she tasted each coin since she couldn't bite down, assuring herself they were real. "This is very generous, young warrior."

"If you remember anything else, send word to Captain Tsar at the garrison. He will see that the message reaches us."

She nodded, and her visitors turned and walked back to the road.

As they walked toward the other houses, Captain Bakaa shook his head. "Human sacrifice,

Sergeant? That's not possible. No god in the land demands human life. I don't believe them."

"I do, Sir. It is true that the Scorpion King, our first leader, outlawed human sacrifice many summers ago, but my father has told me that these sons of Set have been known to practice all the dark arts including such horrible killings."

"Set's bulging buttocks," Bakaa swore. "It turns my stomach."

They learned nothing new from the other houses, although the first woman's neighbors gave them the same story about the child and the head. Returning to the barracks, they shared what they'd learned with Captain Psar.

He sat in with Ko and Captain Bakaa as Ko's trainees made their report. They had learned that a small band of men had been down at the docks bargaining for passage the night before.

Seneferu, one of Ko's men, cleared his throat. "The man who owns the inn on the river told us he looked out his window and saw them in the middle of the night. He thought it unusual for them to wear black robes with hoods, like priests."

"When was this?" Psar asked.

"The night they killed our men," the trainee replied. "He said that they wanted to sail in the full moonlight. Sailing at night is dangerous enough because of sandbars, hippos, and crocs not to mention the changing current. But the captain of a small ship agreed and they left with him and disappeared in the night mist."

"I wonder which direction they took," Bakaa said.

"Toward Memphis," Seneferu answered. "The inn keeper said they probably would escape into the desert red lands."

Ko wiped the sweat from his forehead and then turned to Bakaa. "What can we do, now, Captain? We've learned where the band have been meeting, but now they've gone. The royal family has been alerted but there is not much else we can do, is there?"

Bakaa frowned. "Not unless they rear their ugly heads again. I recommend we return to Awen and join the general if it isn't too late."

Captain Psar appeared genuinely interested now in helping. "We will keep watch, friends. You have exposed these foul men for what they are. We will also have guards alerted all around Thinis to keep watch if they should reappear."

"Good," Bakaa said. "Then we'll sail in the morning if we can find a ship."

That evening, the men of Psar's garrison and young trainees shared a great feast of chicken, fish, and plenty of beer.

As Ko settled down for the night, he said to Bakaa, "We may not have captured the sons of Set, but the local garrison and the palace are on the alert. They'll know what to do."

"I agree, Highness. We have now proven these evil men exist and we must do all we can to bring them to justice." He grunted and shifted on his cot. "I am troubled, however, by the images of other children shedding their blood for their sacrifices."

Ko rolled over on his stomach and looked across the room at his leader. "What about our fallen brothers, Captain?"

"They have begun their journey to the priests at the House of the Dead. After the seventy days of preparation they will be taken to their villages for burial."

"Good. I really liked those two."

"They were good men."

Ko closed his eyes and the captain blew out the oil lamp. The usual noises of men settling down in the other rooms of the barracks soon diminished.

As his mind began to close down, Ko was disturbed to find images of his friends lying on the floor of the dark tunnel. He had bloodied his hands when he checked to see if they were alive, and it took him awhile to wash it off when they got back. A child's skull entered his thoughts and he turned over on his cot.

Suddenly, angry shouts and cries of surprise brought Ko and Bakaa out into the hallway.

"What is it? Ko demanded.

"Someone's shot an arrow into the door of our room," one of the trainees shouted.

"It carried a message," another man said as he handed it to the captain.

Ko looked over Bakaa's shoulder and gasped.

The bottom of the paper had been signed with the black mark of Set.

8

Ko's heart raced when he recognized the mark. Captain Bakaa read the message aloud:

Set knows the steps of Akhom's son

"How is this possible?" Bakaa growled. "If the black-hooded men left by ship, then it means there are still followers of Set here in Thinis."

"Give me the arrow," Psar said.

Bakaa handed it to him.

"It's one of ours. Look at the fletching. Those feathers come from this garrison."

"Then it must belong to one of your own men, Captain," Ko said.

"What? You accuse me?" Psar shouted. He headed for Ko but the other trainees blocked his path.

Bakaa said, "Stand down, Psar, unless you want the king to execute you and your men for touching the royal person."

Psar cursed and stormed out of the barracks, but none of his men left with him.

One of Psar's sergeants knelt and saluted. "Hail, Prince Ako, blood of the king's blood."

The other men, including the prince's unit, recited the loyalty part of their oath as soldiers.

Ko raised his fist high above his head, "Long live King Djed son of the great Aha."

The men stomped their feet in agreement.

Bakaa stood next to the prince. "How can we find who shot the arrow?"

"It's impossible sir," one of Psar's men said shaking his head. "We were all in our beds when it happened."

One soldier objected. "That's not true. The captain's cousin left for the latrine. He wasn't with us."

Psar's men looked around the room. "He's not here. Has anyone seen him?" another asked.

One of the young soldiers ran outside and returned a few moments later. "Their horses are gone, Captain."

"Psar's too?" Bakaa asked.

"Yes, sir."

Pandemonium broke out and Bakaa stood on a chair to get the soldiers' attention. "Listen to me. You have nothing to fear from us. If Psar and his cousin did this, it doesn't mean you were involved. Now let's go into the common room, sit down and talk it over calmly."

When they were together, Bakaa asked, "Who is next in command?"

"I am," the biggest man in the garrison, replied. "Oba, Sir."

"Good. We must try to sail for Memphis tomorrow. In the prince's presence—and he represents the king—I promote you to Sergeant."

Once again, the men stomped their feet in approval.

"For now, let's get some rest and then tomorrow you can all help us find a ship."

The next day, Ko and the men from his unit arranged with a merchant ship to carry them to the capital. It would only take them two days to reach Memphis because of the strong current flowing to the Great Sea.

When the ship docked in the great city the sun was setting and it was decided the men would sleep on board.

Captain Bakaa, however, would ride with Ko to the palace.

The moon had just slipped above the horizon as the two riders rode through the streets.

"Do you know where we are, Ko?" Bakaa asked. "I'm all turned around."

"Don't worry Captain, we're almost there."

When they reached the wall around the king's palace, Ko and the officer reined in their horses at the main gate.

"Halt," a guard yelled from the dark.

Ko and Bakaa dismounted and stood beside their horses.

"What is the word?" the guard asked.

"I don't know, Guardsman. It changes every day and I've been gone from home for several months."

"Silence. Give the word or be arrested."

Bakaa whispered, "Let's go. They don't recognize you."

"Arrest us, Guardsman. Do your duty," Ko ordered.

The guard drew his sword and indicated the two intruders move inside the gate. He called for another guard to help him.

It was dark inside the guard post and Ko knew the men would have difficulty recognizing him without his narrow crown. To protest that he was a prince would get him nowhere and they would eventually see who he was.

"Into the cell," the guard ordered, pushing the two prisoners inside. It smelled of previous residents, and there were flies everywhere.

The clanking of the metal key turning in the lock caused Bakaa to groan. "You are certain you are a prince, aren't you, Ko? You've not been lying to us? Why didn't you show them your royal mark?"

"I didn't know the password, and should not have been let in. The guard is doing what he should. Relax, friend, we'll soon be out of here."

When no one came they finally fell asleep on the dirty straw matrasses.

Early the next morning, they were awakened by two men talking outside their cell.

"Who have you arrested and why, Rua?" one voice demanded.

"They arrived on horseback, Sergeant, but didn't know last night's password. I threw them into a cell. You told us to be careful of strangers around the palace."

"Open the cell. Let me look," the sergeant said.

Ko stood facing the door to the cell but when the captain entered, he turned around slowly so the man could see the royal seal on his neck.

"Gods!" the captain shouted. "Turn around please."

Ko turned back to face him.

The sergeant fell on one knee. "Prince Ako! Forgive us, Highness. This fool will be punished."

"Do not concern yourself, Sergeant. Your name is Kasa, is it not?"

"Oh, please forget my name, Highness."

Ko laughed. "You have nothing to fear from me. Do not punish the guard. He did the right thing. I didn't know the password." He turned to Bakaa. "This officer is my colleague from the training garrison at Awen. We need to see the king on an urgent matter."

"Of course, my Lord. But first, follow me to my apartment where you can wash up."

"Lead on."

Afterward, Ko led Bakaa along the polished stone corridors to the royal apartments in the center of the palace. It was early morning, and servants were everywhere preparing the palace for the new day.

It was Merneith who saw him first.

"Ko," she shouted, running and embracing him.

"Hugging her and spinning her around, he said, "Merry, it is so good to see you."

"It's been so long, Ko. This is such a boring place without you."

Bakaa knelt on one knee and saluted her.

"Who is this?" she asked.

"This is Captain Bakaa, the officer of my unit. Be nice to him."

The girl turned to him and smiled. "Welcome, Captain. Because you are my cousin's friend, you are especially welcome."

"Thank you, Highness," was all Bakaa managed.

Ko smiled because his friend was uncomfortable—first for being in the king's palace, and now in a princess' presence. "I'll be back, Merry. We must see the king. It's very important."

"All right, you promised, remember."

Ko and Bakaa continued along the corridor until they reached the golden ornate doors of the king's residence. The beautifully sculpted portal bore a large cedar carving in the image of Horus, the great falcon.

Captain Nebi, in charge of the guards, met them and saluted. "Highness, welcome home."

"I must see the king, Captain. It is urgent."

"These are dangerous times. I hope you bring him good news," Bakaa said.

"Quite the contrary, my friend. But he needs to hear what is happening."

Nebi waved his hand, and the door opened.

"Wait here Captain," Ko said. "Nebi is a friend."

Bakaa nodded and waited beside him.

Ibi, the king's steward came to meet him. "Highness?"

"I must see my uncle, Ibi. It is a matter of life and death in the very real sense."

"Of course, Highness. I will tell him you are here."

Ko took a seat on one of the deeply cushioned divans in the foyer. He felt anxious for the first time as he waited to see his uncle. Would the king realize the importance of what he was about to tell him? Perhaps he was too young for the king to take him seriously.

His majesty walked into the foyer wearing a long, thin white robe. "Ko, welcome. What brings you home and so early in the morning?"

"Majesty, our lives are in danger—all of us. May I tell you what we've learned these last days about the sons of Set?"

Djed didn't respond, but walked to the door. "Captain Nebi," he called. When the officer came at once he said, "Send someone for Akhom and then you are to come in as well."

Bakaa saluted and hurried off.

"Ko said, let my Captain come in too, Great One."

The king waved his hand giving permission. He scowled and crossed his arms. "You have spoken the name I have forbidden to be uttered in my presence. I should throw you in prison."

"I spent the night in your prison, Majesty, thanks to your guards."

"Explain yourself."

"I think I will do so when Father arrives, Uncle. He'll want to hear as well."

"Enough of your impertinence, Ko. If you don't tell me, my wrath will fall on you and your family."

"Very well but the evil followers of the name we were never to speak, are in Thinis and have killed two of my men."

"No, say it isn't so. I can't believe it is starting again. Why are the gods doing this to me?" He collapsed onto one of the divans, a hand to his forehead.

Ko sat on a cushioned bench, not knowing what to say.

Captain Nebi entered. "Akhom is coming, Majesty."

"Good. We will meet out on the veranda. I don't wish to disturb the queen with this news."

The door opened again and it was Akhom who moved inside, catching his breath. When he saw his son, his furrowed brow showed alarm.

"Bring Bakaa, and the other captain, and follow me," the king ordered.

The king led them onto the large veranda and took the chair he always used near the wall overlooking the city and the river. "All right, Ko, tell us what is happening."

"Majesty, Captain Bakaa and I, along with ten trainees came to Thinis two days ago. Our roommate was murdered by the Setites but we caught the killer. He wore the mark of the evil god and we were able to force from him the names of their leader and other members living in Thinis. It must be the same band who killed your father, Majesty, our beloved Aha."

Ko's father frowned and nervously cleared his throat—something he always did when upset. He spoke just above a whisper. "It can't be happening, Majesty. If so, the words I spoke on the day of King

Aha's entombment were not true. The sons of Set are not dead."

King Djed shook head. "We all believed it was true, my friend."

Captain Nebi said, "Why would they kill a trainee in your room, my prince?"

Ko said, "Digger looked so much like Jet, the killer thought he was your son and strangled him."

"Wait," Nebi interrupted. "Someone tried to kill the crown prince?"

"Yes, Captain. Our bunkmate was killed by mistake."

"That still doesn't explain what sent you to Thinis, Son," Ko's father said.

Ko explained by giving a detailed account of the events of the past four days.

"Is that everything," the king asked.

"No, Majesty. Two days ago, as we were going to bed in the barracks in Thinis, an arrow struck a door where we were staying. There was a message attached which said, 'Set knows the steps of Akhom's son.'"

The king's face reddened. He sat up straighter in his chair and had trouble controlling his anger.

"We searched the barracks, Majesty and discovered that the arrow came from Captain Psar's men—they could tell by the feathers. His men said, he and his cousin had not been in the barracks at the time. But they left the garrison on horseback. This means there are followers of the dark lord—forgive me, Majesty—in the king's army."

Nebi said, "We have tightened our security here at the palace, Majesty when we received word of what had happened in Thinis. I understand Prince Ako spent the night in your majesty's prison."

"Oh?" Akhom said.

"Yes, Father. I had no crown and did not know the password. Nebi's men caught us—as they should have."

The king stood and paced around the veranda. Above them, the azure-blue sky and morning sun showed the promise of a perfect day. However, the look of gloom on his majesty's face did not suggest such optimism.

"My son must come home at once," he said. "They have tried to kill him so he is not safe."

"He can't come home, Great One," Ko said. "He's gone into the northern desert with General Mereruka's army. They left at the beginning of this week."

"Do we know the name of the leader of these assassins?" the king asked.

"He is known by his followers only as 'the Jackal,' but we think it is Setau," Ko answered.

"I must think on these things. You will stay with your family until we have a plan, Ko. As angry as I may be, I am grateful to you for reporting this. I will send Bakaa to go back with you to bring him home."

"Yes, Majesty," Ko said.

The king stood and left them.

Lord Akhom, led Ko and the two captains down the hallway toward the door that led to the connecting houses.

Ko stopped abruptly. "I forgot, Father. I promised Merry I would visit her after I spoke with the king."

Akhom nodded, and he and the other two men continued on to Akhom's home.

The prince walked back to the king's apartment and told the steward Princess Merry had sent for him.

"She's with her Majesty, Highness. I'll take you to them."

Ko followed and found the queen and her daughter sitting in the shade of the large palms in a pleasant green oasis-like garden.

Merry saw him and rushed toward him.

He embraced her. "You are getting taller, Highness. You've grown even more than when I last saw you."

She released him. "I want to hold your hand," Merry said.

Ko let her and she led him to a bench near the queen.

"Sister," he said, bowing his head formally.

She stood and embraced him gently. "Come, sit beside me."

Ko followed her and sat down. Merry jumped up, hurried back into the palace, and returned with a beautiful cat. It was tawny in color and stripes had started to appear on its back.

"I call her Zee-zee, because she is precious to me. Thank you for sending her all the way from Awen. I love her so much. She reminds me of you and how you care about me."

"Hello Zee-zee," Ko said running his hand along the kitten's back. "She's grown since last I saw her. I'm glad Bata was able to reach you in the palace. I wanted you to know I was thinking of you."

"Meowwrrr…" it said and jumped onto his lap.

Merry's cheeks had turned a darker pink. "She likes you."

"I'm glad. She's beautiful."

"Will you come visit me tomorrow?" the princess asked.

"It all depends on your father, Princess. He wants me to go back to Awen and bring your brother home."

"No, no. Not that horrible baboon again. Can't you keep him?"

"Merry," her mother said. "Be a princess."

Ko stood. "I will promise to come to you when we are back, Lady Merneith."

Merry hugged him and he said, "You must excuse me, Majesty, Princess. Mother will never forgive me if I don't spend time with her."

"Then you must go, Brother. It is good to see you again."

Ko took Merry's hand and kissed it before leaving the garden.

As he hurried away, he heard the princess declare to her mother, "I'm going to marry Ko, Mother. Begin the arrangements."

9

After two days with the king, Ko, and Captain Bakaa would sail north and join with General Merseruka's advance into the desert. When they reached Awen, they learned that the general and his army had sailed for Tharo on the Great Sea above the river delta. Ko would leave his fellow trainees at the Academy and then travel with Captain Baakaa into the desert.

"I want Sabu to come with me," Ko told the captain.

"Not unless he's an excellent archer and swordsman, Highness."

"He's the best, Captain. Ask the men of the academy."

"Very well, but he'll be your aide and will have orders to watch over you."

"I will be proud to have him at my side."

"Agreed. We'll sail in the morning."

When Ko and Sabu arrived at the dock, the Wind of Shu was already loaded and Captain Bakaa growled, "You're late."

"You said sun-up, sir," Sabu protested.

"The rays of Ra's glory have been seen for some time now. I will not tolerate this lack of discipline.

Angered by the Captain's words, Ko said, "We will hold you to the same standard, Captain. Be more precise when you give orders."

Bakaa burst out laughing. "Good. You're not afraid of me."

Ko grinned and hurried up the gangway with Sabu at his heels. Throwing their bags down on deck, he asked, "How long will the voyage take?"

Sabu said, "The captain told me two days up through the delta until we reach the port city of Tharo."

Ko put a foot up on the lower railing and stared at the passing countryside. "I've never been beyond the sacred river."

Bakaa said, "Most of your countrymen have not traveled this far north."

Sabu said, "This ship looks stronger than most of our ships."

"You have a good eye, Toadlet. Some of these planks have been secured with wooden pegs like the Phoenician vessels that sail the Great Sea. Our ships normally use bitumen—that black sticky substance— to seal the planks which are then tied by ropes to secure them. Wooden pegs hold them tighter and longer."

The young men toured the ship including a visit below. When they returned to the upper deck, Ko asked, "Why didn't we bring horses, Captain? We saw two below."

Bakaa sat on one of the wooden benches near the railing and scratched his chin. "They're good in the delta where the soil is firm. They're not as good on sand."

Sabu went off to talk with some of the other passengers. Ko walked forward and stood at the bow railing. He loved the smell of the river and the wind on his face. An occasional splash of spray wet his hair and he ran his fingers through it like a comb.

Everything was greener as the ship followd the eastern-most branch of the river. Papyrus and bullrushes mixed in with floating water hyacinths covered the riverbanks. The bulbous roots enabled the invasive plant to float on the surface of the water. Brilliant tourqouise kingfisher birds plunged into the water only to soar away time and time again with small silver fish in their beaks.

Crew and passengers enjoyed broiled fish, fresh bread and jars of beer kept cool by hanging them over the side of the ship in the water.

At night under the stars, the ship's captin showed them how to navigate using the stars in the dark canopy overhead. "Seafaring peoples use knots on a rope to mark the stars and navigate—I find it amazing."

A crewman brought out a lute and provided music for the men who sang and danced. Unfortunately, their movements became more and more erratic as their consuption of beer increased.

By early afternoon of the third day, they reached Tharo. Ko and Sabu marveled at the large ships anchored in the harbor. At the local garrison, Bakaa and his younger colleagues were warmly received. However, that all changed as soon as the men discovered the royal tatoo on the back of Ko's neck. They became nervous and wary of his presence.

Captain Ainu, the officer in charge of the garrison said, "There are three horses waiting for you as per the general's orders."

Bakaa raised his eyebrows. "Oh? I was told that horses were not good in the desert."

"Not true my friend. They do well, provided they have grain and water. Remember for you too, water is your life-blood in the red lands."

"When did the general's army pass through?" Ko asked.

"Last week, and I never saw so many ships at one time. There were warriors everywhere and they ate everything in sight. The local fishermen couldn't keep up with their demand. We were glad when they left."

"Are we three on our own?" Ko asked.

"No, Highness. Before the general left, he received a messenger pigeon from Thinnis telling him you were coming. There is a platoon of thirty archers accompaning you. He left them to escort you to his camp." Aniu paused to wipe the sweat from his forehead.

Ko noticed his frown and the man became nervous or embarassed. "What else, Captain?"

"The general said it was his duty to keep both princes from harm."

"Ah," Ko sighed. "I share his concern now that we know there are Setites out there who want the crown prince dead."

"Who would attempt such a thing?"

"The followers of the god of the storm and darkness have returned, Captain, and are killing again," Ko told him.

"Curses on them," the officer growled. "We thought they'd been destroyed."

Sabu said, "They are like the sickness that flies on the wind and returns every four or five years. We need to wipe them out for good this time."

Captain Ainu said, "Rest yourselves now since you will travel only at night. You leave before sunset. My men have prepared rooms for you in the barracks. Rest well."

At dusk, Ko and Sabu followed Captain Bakaa and the archers out of the city. They kept to the seashore north and then turned west, toward the vast land of the desert. The general also left one of his scouts to journey with them. When they reached the edge of vegetation, he took over and showed them the tracks of the army they would follow for the next week.

Ko thought they'd soon be in sand, but for as far as he could see, there were rocky stretches in the arid land ahead. Ko, Sabu, and Bakaa were on horseback, but kept pace with the men on foot. As darkness fell, Ko dismounted and led his horse by the reins alongside the rest of the men.

One of them asked, "What's a prince doing out in this stinking place?"

"A worthy question," Ko replied, keeping his eyes straight ahead. "I want to save my cousin, the crown prince from being murdered."

His words caused a stir among the archers. He knew they were also sizing him up, so he starightend his back and kept pace with them. "The evil band who killed Prince Djet's grandfather, the Great King Aha, has returned and threatens the royal family."

At the mention of Aha's name, the men shouted as one voice, "We honor his name."

The scout Hapu, rode over to them. "Silence! Voices carry a long way in the desert."

Ko asked, "How are you called?"

"I am Hapu, Highness."

"Good, you know who I am. Captain Bakaa is in charge of our crossing the desert."

"Not so, Highness. The general left me in charge of you. I am the only one who can get you across the sands. You will obey me or die. You will eat when I eat, drink when I do and obey me or you can kiss your lives a fond farewell."

No one talked to Ko like that. He felt his cheeks flush and was glad it was too dark for anyone to see.

Raising his voice, Hapu continued. "We will travel through the night—when it is cool, and sleep during the day. Heat and lack of water are our biggest killers. You have been given a kaftan to wear. It gets cold here at night as you will soon find out."

"There is no moon to see by," Ko said. "How can you find the way?"

"By the sand and the stars, Prince. Never fear."

They took out their robes from their saddlebags. Sabu took a small loaf of flat bread from his pack and shared it among the four of them. The archers did the same—drinking only a small amount of water at Hapu's insistence.

As Ko stood beside his horse, a cool desert breeze blew across his face. He raised his shoulders so the robe could cover his neck. The air was cold.

Hapu walked up behind him. "Desert people wear their robes day and night. They also protect from the sun. You'll be glad for them."

"Thank you, Hapu. We hope to learn your desert skills."

Bakaa joined them. "A fire would feel good."

"No, Captain, never at night. It can easily be spotted miles away. No, we'll prepare our fire in the morning before we sleep. It will be hard to spot and the wind blows away the smoke."

The scout approached the archers. "Are we ready?" When he received agreement from everyone he gave the order, "Move out."

Rather than riding his horse, Ko decided to walk alongside their scout. "Tell us about the gods of the desert winds."

Speaking softly, Hapu said, "In the morning, my Lord. There are jackal's ears out there, perked up trying to hear everything." He moved on ahead alongside Sabu and the others.

"Strange man," Sabu whispered.

"I heard that," Hapu whispered back. "Be silent."

Crossing the desert at night at first seemed impossible, at least until their eyes grew accustomed to the darkness. Stars they knew back home appeared as if to encourage them on. The thin crescent moon appeared again, and its light was enough to see the scout's footprints up ahead.

When it was directly overhead, Hapu raised his hand and everyone stopped. Ahead of them was a large group of boulders and they chose places to rest around them. "Feed and water the horses at the small spring. Everyone take a turn drinking as much as you can—it will be good for your system. We will rest here awhile."

Ko was surprised how thirsty he had become, even in the cold night air.

"Relieve yourselves by twos or more. We don't want anyone picked off by jackals or pursuers." He paused and then said, "There will not be any water for two more days, so ration your water carefully."

It felt good to get off their feet, and even though tempted to talk among themselves, no one broke the scout's rule. After too short a rest, Hapu led them on.

As the light pinks and yellows of the new day splashed across the eastern sky, Hapu led them to a dry riverbed in front of a long granite formation. "There are caves here where we can sleep. Divide yourselves up and someone gather wood for a fire. There are lots of dried acacia branches around. Beware of vipers and cobras, and there are poisonous scorpions everywhere. Go by twos, or threes—never alone."

In the shadow of the large rock formation, Hapu sat down and put his feet up on a flat rock. "Ah," he sighed. "Now, Highness. You asked about the gods of the desert wind."

"Yes, what can you tell us?"

Ko studied their scout who had seen perhaps thirty summers. His head was shaved, and skin deeply bronzed. His brownish-green eyes flashed when he spoke, and a small black goatee added to the length of his pleasant face.

"First, there is Manat, goddess of these red lands. The nomads who live here, believe her star is the first one seen when evening falls. She is the sister of Ta'lah, god of the moon to these people. We might consider her like our Great Isis." He cleared his throat and continued. "The desert people say you can see Manat's image in a sandstorm if you look carefully, but I've never seen her."

"What about the mountain?" Bakaa asked.

"Yes, well, that is a long story. It can wait until tomorrow. We need to sleep now. You know how hard the trail can be, so rest well."

On the morning of the third day, they approached another grouping of boulders—some as big as a house. Hapu showed them a small spring bubbling up from under a large flat black stone. He bent over, sniffed the water, dipped a finger in and tasted it. Only then did he fill his waterskin from the pool and take a drink.

"Never can be too careful for poisons," he said. "This water's safe. Fill your skins to bursting."

"We'll camp here for the day. There are plenty of places to find shade. Archers may hunt by twos, but mark your path so you won't get lost. Large hares make a tasty meal."

It wasn't long before the hunters returned with a dozen of them which were quickly skinned and placed on green acacia sticks over the fire. The aroma of roasted hare made Ko's mouth water.

As Sabu chewed he said, "I didn't think anything would taste as good as fresh fish, but this meat is delicious."

"Why so quiet, Captain?" Ko asked Bakaa.

"I was just thinking how impossible it would have been for us to try to cross the desert by ourselves. I praise the general's scout."

"I agree," Ko said. "Growing up around the palace I always thought old Mereruka was a bit mad. But I am revising my opinion."

After the meal, the travelers found places to sleep among the rocks. The horses had been trained to lie down in such places, and after their grain and water, lay in the shade.

By late afternoon, everyone was up and ready to continue.

"How do you know where to find the army's tracks. Doesn't the wind blow away any trace of them?" Bakaa asked Hapu as they saddled up. "When it becomes totally dark, I can't see their trail."

"You could, Captain, if you knew how."

Bakaa exhaled. "I'm lucky if I can see the ground."

When Ko grew tired of holding his horse's reins, he let go of them. The animal continued to follow the others anyway.

"Trust your horse," the scout said in a quiet voice.

After some time, Ko's horse's ears perked up and it became skittish. He grabbed the reins again.

Hapu approached them and whispered, "There are jackals following us."

Ko could hear their barking yelp in the distance and then the echos bounced all around them.

"Archers at the ready," Hapu ordered. "Kill three or four and they'll have something to eat and leave us alone. Gather in a circle with the horses in the middle. Quickly."

Once in place, Bakaa said to Ko, "You need to be in the middle next to your horse, my friend." When Ko tried to object, the captain raised his hand and Ko fell silent.

A cloud moved away from the face of the moon, and its light allowed them to see the predators circling around them. Ko counted six, but they moved so fast he was unsure if the archers could hit any.

An agonizing yelp and angry growling proved him wrong. There was another cry and their scout's prediction proved true—they began to tear their own kind apart and drag off the pieces.

"Move out," Hapu said in a loud voice. "They'll be back."

In the clear light, they followed their scout. Ko could see where he was headed. A tall moundlike rock formation lay a short distance away. When they reached it, Hapu said, "We can get up on the large flat table of stone and pick off any jackals that come our way. They'll tire of being shot, so don't alarm yourselves."

Climbing up was harder than first thought, but they even managed to help their horses onto the level surface.

"This will not help us when the sun comes up, but for now, we are safe," Hapu assured them.

"Hapu," one of the men shouted his name and motioned for the scout to come over.

Ko and Sabu followed behind him and their eyes grew bigger when they saw the body of a man lying on the ground. Flies buzzed around it even in the moonlight.

Hapu bent over it and then said, "Does anyone know this sign?"

Ko leaned over and groaned. It was the black mark of Set behind the man's ear. "Gods," he sighed.

10

"Gods! He's one of those devils," Ko said. "What's he doing up here?"

Bakaa bent down and turned the body over. "Ah," he said. "There's the reason we found him. See the two puncture marks on his leg—snake bite. From the size of them, I'd say a cobra."

Hapu picked up the man's dagger. "He was here to keep his eye on us and became careless."

The yelping and call of the jackals came closer to the flat rock escarpment. Archers picked them off easily. The pack fell on the fallen and tore them apart.

More arrows reached their mark and the predators ran off with the torn pieces in their jaws.

Hapu said, "Captain, we must find our safe place for the day. The sun will be up soon. Let's go."

Ko and the men followed him down the flat rock due east. Archers carried their weapons at the ready in case of animal attack.

After a short march, they reached a small mountain of black granite. It thrust up from the sand perhaps a hundred cubits high.

"There's water here," Hapu said, "and crevices to sleep in. Clear out any snakes and scorpions before you go in. Do so quickly before the sun's rays reach us."

Ko breathed in the pleasant aroma of wet soil and mossy plants as the men claimed their spots. Two fires were started and a dozen partridges, flushed from their nests, were prepared for roasting. The succulent meat was washed down with cool, clear water. The horses grazed on small patchs of grass growing near the springs. Because of their size, they would be moved throughout the day, following the shadow of the mountain as the sun raced across the sky.

Hapu disappeared as Ko and Sabu prepared to sleep.

Later, when he returned he reported to Bakaa. "The army's tracks are fresher here, Captain. I'd say they're about three days ahead of us."

"That's good news," Sabu mumbled to Ko as he pulled up his hood to shield his head from the morning sunlight. "I'm tired out."

"As am I," Ko said. "I'm going to ride my horse tomorrow."

"Um. . .hum," Sabu mumbled, drifting off to sleep.

Three days later, Hapu left camp and rode on ahead. When the moon was directly overhead, he returned and brought someone with him.

"Jet!" Ko exclaimed. "Over here."

The king's son laughed and shouted—"Ko, another brother toad."

The cousins embraced briefly. "Together again," Jet said, patting Ko on the back.

"It is good to see our Prince Toad is still alive," Sabu said good-naturedly.

"Mount up, friends," Jet said. "The general expects us by sun-up." He turned his horse around and waited for them to join him.

When everyone finished saddling up, the archers marched on each side of them as they headed into the bright moonlight. Horses and men did well on the smooth slate rock blown free of sand by the ever present wind. It made a haunting wail as it blew past them. With hoods up against the cold they were surprised when they reached the summit of a large hill, and the wind disappeared as if by some mysterious hand.

Ko gasped. In the valley beyond, were thousands of campfires of Merseruka's army. They resembled stars in the night. "What a sight," he declared, reining in his horse. They spent a moment taking in the view of comrade warriors spread out as far as they could see.

"Let's hope the Asiatics are as equally impressed with our numbers," Jet said. He urged his horse forward and down the other side of the hill. The sun climbed above the horizon as they reached the camp. Passing through endless rows of warriors, many recognized Prince Jet and called out his name. All were digging in, preparing to sleep during the day. Many had tents made from their blankets and dried branches of the acacia to hold them up.

For Ko, the ride through the army felt like it lasted forever. He had never seen so many of the king's men assembled before. By the time they reached the general's pavilion, the sun had climbed a good distance above the horzon.

General Merseruka's large tent was situated on the edge of an oasis. The general stood in the shade of his tent as they rode up and dismounted. "The gods are good," he said, greeting them.

"We greet you in Horus' name, General Meresuka," Ko responded. "Are we glad to see you."

"Put your horses over there with mine," he said, pointing to a lean-to made of blankets near the water.

Sabu led them to the water's edge.

Ko grapsed the general's forearms in greeting.

The general said, "After you've refreshed yourselves, I am anxious to hear of your encounters with these sons of the underworld."

Inside his tent, the new arrivals removed their kaftans for the first time since leaving the Great Sea. It felt good to move about in just their kilts. They drank their fill of water, and one of the general's aides brought them stale bread.

"We can only offer you cold quail, I'm afarid. We've had our night meal and are prearing to dig in for the day."

When Sabu returned, Ko introduced his friend. Everyone sat cross-legged on blankets, except the general who sat on a folding stool. He yawned and stretched his arms. "I'll be glad when we reach the mountain. We will be able to march during the day again."

Captain Bakaa said, "We found a dead spy from the followers of Set, General. He had the mark on his neck. He must have been following us, but became careless and died of a cobra bite. Finding him means we're being followed."

"Set's bowels," the general exclaimed.

Bakaa nodded to Ko who cleared his throat. "There's more, General. They killed two of my men when our captain took us to Thinnis to flush these vermin out. They were using an old shrine for their meetings and offered children in sacrifice to their god."

Meresurka scowled and ran his hand over his bald head. "If they are this far north, it means the crown prince is their target as we feared. It is good you are here with warriors around you."

Jet nodded. "I only wish my parents and sister were as safe. The royal guards have stepped up security around the palace, but I believe they are still in danger."

The general stood and walked to the flap of his tent, pulling it closed. "Isn't there a retreat or family secret hiding place where the royal family can be safe, Prince?"

Jet scratched his scalp where his braid had almost grown back in."Father has friends in Abydos. They've let us use their villa from time to time when we are there for the burials of family members. It's not very secure, I'm afraid."

The men were silent awhile, and only the yapping of jackals in the distance echoed across the sand.

Sabu timidly said, "My family has a farm up at Pa-Osiris, General. Would that help?"

"What?" Merseruka asked.

"My family has a large farm near the delta where the royal family could be safe until these Setites are finally destroyed."

"Pa-Osiris? I don't know the place. Where is it?" Merseruka asked.

Ko said, "I've been there General. It's north of Memphis on the Western shore of the river before it branches out into the delta."

Sabu added, "It's a beautiful place with a small population. There is also a small garrison which could be strengthened during their stay."

"Hum," the older man said, thinking. "We'd have to get them there secretly. Can't use one of the king's ships or everyone would know." He turned to Bakaa. "What do you think, Captain?"

"It needs more thought, sir. But, the idea is good. If these Setites are everywhere, then they might be able to penetrate the palace and kill his Majesty."

"They could go separately, General, and at night," Ko said. "Some ship's captains are willing to sail at night. The river is deeper there and the danger of hidden boulders or sandbars is less that far north. It can be done."

"And us, so far away," Merseruka grumbled. He sat back on his small stool. "I will send a rider with a message to his majesty."

"No, General," Jet interrupted. "If these assassins stop him, they'll get the plan out of him. It is too risky."

Ko said, "Aren't there trade caravans who pass this way all the time, General?"

The old warrior nodded.

"Then send your man, with nothing written down, with one of the caravans. He could be at the Great Sea in a week, perhaps, and then take a ship home."

The general smiled. "Ah, the wisdom of youth. At my age, ideas do not come as quickly as you young men. What we need now, however, is sleep."

When they left the large tent, they helped themselves to what quail there was still available and chose places to sleep for the day.

Jet said, "Sabu, I want you to be the one to go with the caravan. We trust you to get through to the king."

Ko said, "An excellent idea, cousin. Will you do it, friend?"

Sabu smiled. "Of course, brothers. We toads always come through for each other."

As they ate, and drank the cool water of the oasis, they continued to think how best to plan the escape of the royal family from the capital.

In the palace garden in Memphis, Zeezee purred as she sat on the princess' lap. Merry was painting the colors on a dragonfly she had sketched on a piece of papyrus. Her model buzzed its wings as it balanced precariously on a lotus flower in the garden pool.

"It's beautiful," the queen said as she approached and looked over her daughter's shoulder.

"Meeooowww. . . " the cat said, looking up at the lady.

"Ah, Aziza thinks so too."

"Thank you." She put down her brush and set the papyrus aside. "Don't you think Zeezee has grown?"

The queen bent over to pet the cat. "Indeed she has. She no longer fits in your hand, and she has all of her stripes. She's beautiful and surprisingly well-behaved."

As if to contradict the queen, the cat sat up and began to pat the ruby on the end of the queen's necklace. That made the still beautiful woman laugh and her daughter joined in.

"I have come to tell you, Merry, that we are going on a journey."

"What? In the night?"

"Yes, it is a secret so please listen. No one must know. Father wants us to do what he says. You can only bring Zeezee with you and a few clothes. Nothing else."

"Where are we going?"

Her mother shook her head. "Not even I, queen of all the land, know where it is."

"Oh, it's a mystery. I love mysteries."

The deep voice of her father entered the conversation. "Who said anything about a mystery. This is an adventure."

"How long will we be gone?" Merry asked.

"We don't know. It is in the country, so you will not need fancy dresses or jewelry."

"Hurrah," Merry said. "I love the country." She was silent a moment. "But why must we travel at night?"

"Because I say so, and that is all there is to it." He attempted to tap the top of his daughter's head with a knuckle, but she laughed and ducked out of his way.

"All right. Is this a don't-do-what-I-do but do-what-I-say, adventure?"

It was the king's turn to laugh. "Yes, Daughter Number One."

Merry grinned. "Daughter Number One? You have no other daughters. Please, Father."

"Come, ladies. The servants will help us pack, but they cannot come with us. The guards will keep them here so they cannot tell anyone we have left the palace." He paused. "I'm sorry, but you cannot even choose a servant to bring with you."

They followed him back into the king's apartment and went to their own rooms to prepare for their departure.

Merry could hear someone talking across the courtyard. She opened the curtains in her bed chamber and saw her father in the main living room with someone. A man bowed when her father said something.

"It's Sabu," she whispered to the cat. "Maybe that means Ko is back too." She hurried out of her room and walked toward the living room. Barefoot, she made no noise as she approached the room. Their voices were clear enough and she stopped.

"Do the general and my son think this is the safest place for us? You are certain, Sabu?" the king asked.

"Yes, Majesty. It is my family's farm and you will like it. It is cool in the evenings and there is plenty to do. Your family will return here, healthy and filled with the delights of our land. The farm is where life is as it should be, Majesty."

"You are certain none of these Setites will find us?"

At those words, Merry turned and ran back to her bed chamber.

"Setites," she repeated, picking up her cat and hugging her tightly. "There are people out to get us, Zee. Father's adventure is really an escape."

Later, when the king came by to see how she was doing, Sabu was with him.

"Greetings, Sabu," Merry said.

The young man bowed to her. "You don't seem surprised to see me, Princess."

"I heard you talking to Father, earlier, in the big room."

"Oh?" the king said. "You were listening?"

"I didn't mean to. I wanted to ask him if Ko was with him. That's all."

The king sat on the edge of her bed and made her sit beside him. "Then you know this is serious, Daughter. You of all people should know this. You were kidnapped by them and saw how ruthless they can be."

The princess frowned as she remembered what happened when she was taken from the ship and hidden in the desert.

Her father continued. "There are people out there who want to destroy this family. Sabu has offered his family's farm to us as a hiding place. No one can know."

"I understand," Merry said. "How is Ko, Sabu? I really want to know."

"He and your brother are fine, Highness. They wanted to come with me, but the General thought they would be safer with him."

"I'm glad." She stood and pointed to her leather bags. "I'm ready, Father, see?"

"Good. We'll have the evening meal and then you, Mother and Sabu will go down to the docks and sail away. I'll come later, with the captain of the Guard."

"Who is that you have there?" Sabu asked the princess.

"This is Aziza. She was a gift from Ko."

"Ah, a beautiful name for a beautiful cat. Cherished, isn't that what it means?"

"Yes, and because Ko gave her to me, she is even more loved."

She noticed the smile on Sabu's face, but he couldn't know how she really felt about Ko. That was her own personal secret. And now that she was a woman, it was something she would only share with the one she loved.

After darkness fell, the king accompanied his wife and daughter to the ship. Sabu led the way. Surrounded by royal guards, he led the queen and princess on board a small merchant vessel. The king's guards replaced the crew. Only the captain of the ship remained on board.

The light of a half-moon gave everyone a ghostly appearance as the king embraced his family. "The gods go with you, my dear ones. I will join you tomorrow evening." He kissed them, and walked down the gangway to the dock.

Two guards, serving as ruddermen, steered the ship out into the strong current of the sacred river.

The ship slowly disappeared in the evening mist, and his guards escorted him back to the palace. Looking over his shoulder he whispered, "Horus, protect them," as the ship vanished from sight.

11

In the territory north of the Eastern Desert, General Merseruka's army arrived in the red land of Zin.

The general said, "This area is known as the beginning of what we call Ta Maf Kat—the Land of the Shifting Sand. Some say it also refers to the turquoise stone buried beneath the ground."

"The wind is very strong here," Ko observed.

Merseruka nodded. "The desert people believe each wind is moved by a god. We are approaching the Valley of the Caves. Our people have mined turquoise here for hundreds of years—long before there were kings in Kemet."

A runner rushed toward them. "General. An Asiatic army is advancing toward the caves. Ra Company is preparing to take their positions."

The general shouted, "Trumpets, sound the call to arms. How many are there?" he asked the scout.

"We couldn't see," the man said. "They burrow into the sand like beetles."

"Do they have horses?" Bakaa asked.

"Some do, Captain, but they also ride strange beasts. Ugly looking, with large and round hooves, enabling them to walk easily over the sand. They have tall backs and long necks. Unusual creatures indeed."

"Lead us to the front line, Captain," the general ordered. "The royals will ride with me."

"Now it begins," Ko said to Jet as they saddled their horses. They waited until the general was ready. An aide helped him into his leather armor. Made up of hundreds of overlapping leaf-like leather pieces connected by strong rawhide cords, it was still light, and flexible. He also wore a long kilt of the same pieces to protect his legs. Ko and Bakaa rode behind him.

When they reached Ra Company of a thousand men, the captain rode on ahead to find Major Haka, the commander. He returned with the officer in charge a short time later.

Ko found him extraordinary. A large man, Haka wore no armor and his body was covered with scars, especially across his chest and arms. His shaved head and absent eyebrows made him more imposing. Deeply tanned skin made the white of his large eyes stand out.

Merseruka saluted the commander.

"We have engaged the enemy, General," the officer declared. "Follow me,"

The general and his party rode alongside the commander.

"Who are they?" Merseruka asked.

"They are definitely Asiatics, General, but they do not fight like any we've encountered before. They use curved swords and with more horses, their chariots enables them to move quickly.

Ko remembered from his training that everyone living north of Kemet was called Asiatic.

The clashing of swords and shouting reached them and forced the general to shout, "Carry on Commander."

Hakor saluted and rode back to his men.

"A good warrior," Merseruka said.

Captain Bakaa said, "There is a formation of large stones over there, General—a good place for us to observe the action."

"Lead on," the general said.

Jet grumbled to Ko, "Who wants to observe? I want to fight."

"They can't risk you on the front line, Cousin. Let the army crush them."

Jet cursed, but turned his horse around and followed the general.

In the tranquil country-side at Pa-Osiris, an ordinary merchant vessel approached the dock. The king had arrived dressed in a light-blue tunic and ordinary leather sandals.

Semut met him at the bottom of the gangway. "Greetings, friend."

"A kind welcome, friend," the king replied.

"I am Semut, Chief Farmer of our family's lands." He took the king's bag and led him to the wagon. "Sabu, welcome home Son," his father said, giving him a brief embrace.

"You look well, Father. The gods are good to let me see you again."

His majesty climbed into the wagon and sat on the wooden seat, while Sabu jumped into the back. Semut got up on the other side and took his place next to the king.

"You realize in normal circumstances you would be executed for sitting next to me, or for just being in my presence, for that matter," the king said.

"Of course, friend," the farmer replied. "And in normal circumstances I'd be out plowing my fields instead of waiting in town."

The king was not accustomed to people responding to him so directly. He mumbled,

"But thank you for allowing us to impose on your hospitality."

"Of course, Alim—that is your new name. And don't be offended by it. Alim was the name of a good friend who is no longer with us, and we honor his name. It means wise man."

"I approve," the king replied.

As they rode a while in silence, the king wondered what his father would think if he could see him riding in a country wagon dressed like this. "The queen and princess are well?"

"Both well, Alim. Your daughter is actually better than mine in milking the goats."

"What?" the king exclaimed. "Milking goats? No, no, this is too much."

"Oh, she wants to, my friend. She's become a big helper on the farm. Whether it is hoeing a row of corn, or tying up our long green beans. She's wonderful."

King Djed shook his head. "How much farther to the farm?"

"Not long now, friend Alim. I've been waiting in town day and night for your ship these past three days. May I ask what happened?"

Offended by the question at first, the king responded. "There were too many things to take care of at the palace, and I had to delay my departure several times."

Semut nodded his head. "I understand. While I was in town, I purchased more seed for the summer planting and a new hoe for your daughter."

The king, suddenly overwhelmed by it all, stopped talking. He stared at the countryside and had to remind himself why he was here. As far as he could see, the land was a green patchwork of cultivated fields. Children greeted Semut, and Sabu jumped off and ran alongside them, rejecting their pleas to ride in the wagon.

When they rounded a bend in the road, the farmer said, "Here's my kingdom." He pointed proudly to a large house sitting in the middle of a green carpet of grass. Because wood was so hard to find, it was made of stone and wood was only used to hold up the flat roof. On all sides were long fields of grain. He drove the wagon toward a barn and then reined in the horse. Chickens clucked angrily, disturbed by the noisy wagon. The king looked toward the house as the door swung open and his daughter ran toward him.

"Father, you've made it. We gave up hope."

The queen walked onto the porch and waited for him to approach.

He climbed out of the wagon, rushed up the steps and embraced her, kissing her again and again. "I'm so glad you are both well."

"Come inside out of the sun," she invited.

Another woman brought a basin of water for the king to wash his face and hands. Merry brought him a towel.

"This is Rabiah, wife of our good farmer," the queen said. "My new name is Kebi, given me because I am as busy as a bee since I've been here."

The king smiled. "I know what Kebi means, Wife."

Sabu's mother embraced her son and ran her fingers through his hair. "Welcome home."

"This was the safest place I could think of Mother. I suggested their majesties come here."

Semut said, "And we are honored, Great Ones. We will do all we can to keep you from harm."

The king nodded and embraced his wife again.

"My new name is Shadya, Father," Princess Merry said. "I picked it out myself. It means delight and joy."

"And a perfect name," the king said. "I am now Alim, which means 'wise one,' and I am very pleased to meet all of you." He bowed slowly, and everyone laughed.

Rabiah said, "Food is placed on the table at five by our water clock," she said turning to leave the royals alone.

"Wait. You have a water clock?" the king asked.

"It is something Semut has made for us," Rabiah said. "It amuses him and keeps time quite well." She bowed her head slightly and went into the kitchen.

"I can't believe it," the king said. "I have tried for months to have the wise men of the kingdom build me a water clock, but they have been unable to do so. I must send them to you, Semut."

The farmer smiled. "All you need is a bucket with a small hole in it and markings for the hours outside. Water seeping out does the rest." He and Sabu turned and left the room.

The king sat on a large comfortable cushioned chair. "Look at you, Merry. Dirty fingernails and you're barefoot. I am so sorry you have had to suffer here. You are becoming a peasant."

His daughter laughed. "You mustn't call me Merry, Father. I'm Shadya. You never know who might be listening."

The king looked at his wife sitting on the small divan near him. "What has happened to your beautiful hair, Beloved? It saddens me to see you so."

The queen frowned and ran her hands over her hair she had braided herself. "I like it this way, Husband. It is comfortable and cool when working outdoors."

The king had to admit they appeared healthy. Their skin was turning a beautiful bronze in just these few days outdoors. "Where has Zeezee gone? Have you lost her?"

The princess ran from the front room and into her bedroom.

"Here she is," she said walking back out. "She's too fat from eating mice and was sleeping on my bed."

"Meowwwwrrr," the cat objected at being disturbed.

The king said, "Well, we're together at least. Tell me now what you think about having to hide away on a farm."

The queen smiled. "I love it here. We have no servants, but don't really need them. I feel alive. Out here, the fragrances of the flowers and plants make me smile. The food is beyond anything our cooks could prepare. Rabiah is a genius in the kitchen and I am learning to sew and mend my own clothes."

Merry walked over and sat on the arm of the king's chair. "I am learning to do so many things. The children have made me welcome and they think I'm a poor city girl who doesn't really know much about life. I think they're right. Life here is so much happier than back at the palace." The king scowled and she stopped talking.

"Well, my only concern has been for our safety and I see now that Captain Bakaa had the right idea." He paused and had a faraway look. "My only concern now is for our Jet, so far from us."

The heat in the desert of Zin was unbearable. Ko dismounted and sat under the shadow of one of the large boulders thrown down by the gods eons ago. Jet did the same and they stared out across the field of battle. Great clouds of dust rose from the desert where the two armies fought hand-to-hand.

"Our men outnumber the enemy," Jet observed. "There's a blue banner. A division of Hakor's men are going around to the left through that opening."

The pressure of Merseruka's warriors behind was too great and his numbers overwhelming. Like the bursting of a dyke they forced the opening, and a solid mass of the fighting men rushed through the enemy's ranks.

"A green one has been raised," Ko said. "Another division is heading in the opposite direction. They'll surround them easily."

The general joined them, standing between the two princes. "That's the end of it. I told you Hakor was a good officer."

Captain Bakaa rode over and dismounted. "It's all over but the cleaning up. It is unfortunate there were so few of them. But I still don't understand what they were fighting for. We have trade agreements with these desert tribes to mine their turquoise. Why fight a battle for the caves and mines?"

They drank from their waterskins and waited for Hakor to send the general news of his victory. The sun had moved from mid-morning and now stood directly overhead when the commander of Ra Company arrived. He was not alone. Tied to the back of one of the strange desert beasts was a wounded Asiatic.

Hakor dismounted and saluted. "They have been defeated, General. This man is one of their officers. I thought you would like to question him before we allow him to fall on his sword."

"Very good. Ride back with us to my pavilion, Commander. We will celebrate you and your men. But for now let's get out of the sun."

Hakor saluted again, climbed on his horse, tied the reins of the desert beast to his saddle and headed back toward Merseruka's camp.

Using the hoods of their kaftans, the royals covered their heads and followed.

Back at camp, everyone drank their waterskins empty and filled them again from old wells dug before Kemet was a nation. Archers had been hunting, and the aroma of roasted antelope permeated the camp.

Soldiers built fires in anticipation of the cold nights. A much larger one in front of the general's pavilion was also prepared. Major Hakor, now washed and wearing a clean warrior's kilt, arrived at the general's tent.

"I've brought the prisoner, General," he said.

"Bring him forward. We still have time before the feast,"

Hakor motioned for his two men to lead in the prisoner.

Jet and Ko sat on folding stools next to the general. Ko's studied the prisoner, who wore only a loincloth. He was forced to his knees in front of the general.

"Can he speak our tongue?" Merseruka asked.

"No, General," Hakor replied. "I've brought Sergeant Ibi with me to translate."

"Good. Ask him who he is and why did he attack us?"

The Asiatic's right eye was swollen shut. Blood from a cut on his forehead covered it. "Water," the man gasped.

Hakor waved his hand and an aide upended a waterskin over the man, who opened his mouth and eagerly gulped it down. "I am Sahail, leader of my tribe."

"Why have you attacked us?" the general asked again.

"This is our land," the man replied. "You anger our gods of the desert winds by your presence. You do not belong here. Our gods protect these lands and you will pay a heavy price for your intrusion."

Ko whispered to the general. "This man sounds educated, General. He speaks too well for a soldier. I believe he may be something more."

Captain Bakaa nodded. "I agree. May I ask a question?"

The general nodded.

Bakaa approached the prisoner and asked, "Who are these gods of the desert winds?"

The interpreter translated the response. "You cannot speak of these gods, foul river dwellers." Ibi turned to the captain, "He also uses special words for his gods. I don't know how to translate them."

"I see. Ask him where do these gods come from?" Bakaa asked.

The prisoner pointed out across the desert. "The holy mountain calls them and they come. They will come for you too, non-believers!"

"Enough," Merseruka said. "Tie him up. We will celebrate the feast and speak to him in the morning. See that he does not harm himself. I think he knows more than he is telling us."

"Yes, General," Hakor said. He motioned for his two aides to take the prisoner away.

Ko turned to Jet. "What do you think? He must be more than a soldier."

"I agree, Cousin. He may be a prophet or holy man out here in the wind and sand. He may be harmless, but I think we should find out more about him."

That evening, the general's men settled into caves dug by the turquoise miners. They ate succulent roasted antelope, and freshly killed desert quail. The commanders of the six companies were the general's guests, but he gave special attention to Ra Company and its men.

"Where will the army go from here, General?" Captain Bakaa asked.

"We go north toward the mountain."

Jet said, "On our ancient maps of the desert, General, they show that there is nothing but a long range of mountains resembling a backbone heading north into Ta Maf kat. How can you find one particular mountain?"

"We are still uncertain, Highness. I was hoping our mysterious prisoner could enlighten us."

Jet glanced at his cousin and said so only they could hear, "Let's slip away. Maybe with the interpreter we can learn something from the prisoner the general can use."

They left the celebration and walked to Hakor's camp. They were met by a troubled Ibi. "Something bad has happened and when the general finds out, we're all going to die!"

"What is it?" Ko asked.

Ibi was trembling. "The prisoner's killed himself. He must have found a thin, sharp shard of turquoise in the sand and cut his own throat. The blue-green stone is still in his hand."

12

Ko bent over the dead body of the prisoner. The man's legs were still staked into the sand, as was his left arm. The leather strap on his right arm was broken, and the turquoise shard was in his right hand. "No, no, no! Look behind his right ear. It's not possible. There's the cursed mark."

Jet became alarmed and frantically looked around. "Then he was after me, Ko." He paused and looked back at the body. "How could an Asiatic warrior bear that mark?"

"I'll go bring the Captain."

Shaken by what they'd discovered Jet panicked. "No, you are not leaving me here. We'll go together."

"All right."

They rushed back to the caves and found Bakaa speaking with Major Hakor.

Jet interrupted them. "Excuse us, Commander. We need the Captain urgently. Something has come up."

Hakor nodded and Bakaa followed the two young men a few steps away. "Why are you interrupting me? What is it?"

Ko spoke softly. "The prisoner is dead, Captain. He killed himself."

"No! That's not possible." Bakaa began to pace back and forth. "But he had no weapon. The guards took everything away from him. Set's foul breath! The general will have our heads."

"Rightfully so, Captain," Jet said. "Come and look at the body."

Bakaa followed them back. He bent down and examined the sharp piece of turquoise covered in blood. He looked behind the man's ear and gasped when he saw the Setite mark. "I can't believe it." Aggravated, he paced again. "But he's not one of us. How is it possible? These people do not worship Set."

Ibi, who had stayed with the body said, "What will you tell the General? I would recommend not telling him right away. We will have a few hours of life at least before he executes us."

"Of course he'll kill us," Bakaa said. "We were responsible for the prisoner. It is even more complicated because he will want to know how we let this happen. What can we tell him?"

They sat on the ground staring at the body. A cold wind blew in from the north and Ko shivered. He pulled his robe closer and blew warm air on his hands, rubbing them together. He said, "I know I'm still young and inexperienced, Captain, but it seems to me there is a Setite in the army. The Crown Prince isn't safe here either. I can't help but feel the army is not the best place for him."

"What? Why would you say such a foolish thing, Highness? Our men all know about the threat of the Setites. If anyone had such a brand on them, his comrades would know and report him. I don't think the crown prince has any reason to worry."

Jet scowled. "That doesn't make me feel any better. I agree with Ko. Someone in the army did this. The prisoner did not kill himself."

"I think this warrior was not meant to be captured and one of his colleague Setites silenced him," Ko said.

Bakaa stood and walked a few steps away from the body. He turned and whispered. "But it is too ridiculous to think this battle took place just so a now dead warrior with the mark of Set would have a chance to kill the prince. It's not only a wild idea, but not possible. Jet has never been alone at any time. One of us has always been with him."

Jet rubbed his hands up and down his arms. "It's too cold out here. I am going back to the general's fire."

Feeling defeated, he and the others walked back toward the caves. Ibi didn't go with them. "I'll see if I can find out if my men saw anything unusual in the night."

Bakaa said, "Let's wait until the general's eaten, before telling him."

Jet said, "It doesn't matter when you tell him. We're doomed."

A lonely figure sat on the farmer's porch. Puffy white clouds overhead menaced the clear sky as they floated south from the Great Sea. A dragonfly, its luminescent wings reflecting the light in a myriad of colors, rested on the man's big toe. The ruler of the united kingdoms of Upper and Lower Kemet wiggled his foot, sending the creature on its way.

The king continued to refuse to take part in farm life. He spent his days sitting in the shade close to the house. His daughter knew his moods when he was like this, and he was glad she was wise enough to leave him alone.

This morning, he stared for hours at three falcons circling on rising thermal air currents above the house. He called to them—"Horus, hear your son.

Find and destroy these cursed followers of the god of darkness, your greatest enemy. Protect my son, Jet, next to sit on your throne. We worship and honor you."

The birds cried out to each other and he believed the falcons were speaking to him somehow. One of them dove toward the palms where he was sitting and dropped something on the ground close to him.

Long pink branches of a nearby oleander moved, making him turn his head.

He stood and walked over to see what the falcon god had given him. "Aha," he exclaimed, picking up the gift from the heavens. "Come out, Merry, you scamp. I know you've been spying on me."

The princess laughed and ran over to see what he had in his hand.

"It's the head of a young cobra—one of the symbols of the god of darkness. You see, Merry, Horus-Ra has defeated the evil god. This is a sign from him that we will be victorious."

"A good omen indeed, Alim," she said emphasizing his name. "Does this mean you'll take more of an interest in the farm?"

He ignored the question. "I must be careful of this. It still has its poison." He called to one of the farmhands to bring a shovel and bury it. "Be careful," he warned the man. "Do not touch the fangs, they can still kill." Wiping his hands on his tunic, he patted his daughter on the head. "You're almost as tall as me. Did you know that?"

"No. I have no time to look in polished copper mirrors. I'm off to milk the goats." She kissed him gently on the cheek and hurried away.

Watching her go, the king realized her metamorphosis into a woman had been too fast. He would soon lose her to some young man he probably would not approve of. He walked back to the house, entered the bedchamber and picked up his linen nemes. Scowling at the simple head covering, he put it on. It would at least protect him from the sun.

Several farmhands were working in the field near the house and he joined them.

One of them asked, "Feeling better, Alim? Semut said you had been unwell."

"Yes, I am better. What can I do?"

The worker gave him a sack that had a cloth handle to fit over the shoulder. Slinging it on, he began to snap ears of corn off one by one, dropping them into the bag. When it was full, he walked to the wagon at the end of the field, emptied it and walked back to the next row.

After a while, he said, "This is hard work, isn't it?" He wiped sweat from his forehead and marveled that he was actually working.

"It's hard at first because you live in the city and are not used to it," another said. "It will get easier. You are doing very well."

The king grinned. If his old chamberlain could see him and hear the worker's praise, he would be astonished.

That evening, as he washed for supper, he was careful with the blisters on his hands. It was a new discomfort for him, and one of the workers showed him how to apply ointment to them. His neck too was sunburned and hurt when his tunic touched it.

At the table that evening, he felt he really deserved the food placed in front of him. He couldn't explain the satisfaction he was experiencing, but it was pleasant.

Merry said, "Mother. Alim picked the corn on our table."

The queen smiled. "Let me see your hands, Husband."

The king raised them, and she smiled. "Well done."

Semut, who sat at the head of the table, said, "I must say, however, friend Alim, that red nose doesn't look good. Put on some palm oil in the morning. We can't have you looking like you've been over-indulging our wine."

The king laughed. "I will."

His daughter beamed at him and raised a second ear of corn and began to nibble.

The farmer said, "I'm going into town in the morning, everyone. Care to ride with me, Alim?"

The king thought about it a moment. "Is that wise?"

Semut nodded. "We'll talk about it later."

The king savored each bite of food. Sabu and three of the farmer's children also ate with them. In addition to the fresh corn on the table, Semut's wife had prepared roast chicken, plenty of green and red beans, large peppers, and fresh yellow apples or tangerines for dessert. The aroma rivaled any food served in the palace dining room.

Later, he, Sabu and Semut were alone on the front porch. As they drank cool homemade beer, the farmer said, "You don't have to worry about going to town, my friend. None of our farmhands have recognized you or your family. I thought you might enjoy a change."

The king said, "I would like to go but I just don't want to put my family in danger if I'm recognized."

"Do any of the men in our local garrison know you are here, Majesty?" Semut asked.

"No. They've been told that I was an important merchant from the capital taking a rest with his family. That's all."

"Let me ride along with you," Sabu said. "I'll have my short sword under my tunic. We can never be too careful."

Semut smiled. "Good. I must purchase a few things. We need sea salt for the cattle and wheat seed from lands north of the Great Sea. Rabiah also wants new cloth to make dresses."

The men fell silent, enjoying the peaceful end of the day. When the women joined them, the king saw

Merry and sucked in his breath. She wore a long light-green robe gathered just under her young breasts. Her hair was swept back and his eyes misted over. She was no longer his little girl.

Her mother was rocking in a chair made from cut-off barrels. "Read to us, Merry," she said.

The princess went inside and returned with a small scroll of parchment and began to read about the adventures of King Narmer, the first king and her great-grandfather. It was the story of the Scorpion King, loved by everyone. As she read, there was a calm stillness and the sweet song of a nightingale gave its accompaniment.

For the king, this was what life was all about. He looked at his wife and she nodded and then smiled. He was certain she had found it too.

To the northeast, in the vast land of Zin, Ko and Jet were troubled by what they had found. A cool breeze lingered so they pulled their kaftans closer.

Ko said, "I've thought about this, Cousin. The assassin must be someone close to the general."

"What? No. It's not possible."

"Listen. No one could have infiltrated our troops and reached that prisoner. They would have been seen by one of us."

Jet nodded. "True enough."

"It had to be a guard, or an officer. No one would suspect them."

"Curse them! What can we do?" Jet asked.

Ko shrugged. "Bakaa must not tell the general about the mark behind the man's ear. Simply tell him what we thought at first—that the man killed himself with the turquoise shard."

"We must get to the general before Bakaa tells him."

They hurried to Bakaa's camp. The officer was meeting with several sergeants and the young men waited courteously for him to finish.

"Oh, there you are," Bakaa said, as he walked toward them. "Do you want to go with me when I tell the general?

"Yes, sir," Ko said. "But we think you shouldn't tell him everything."

"Explain," Bakaa said, his voice showing a growing concern.

Jet explained, and the captain's face changed. "You think it was me?"

Shocked, Ko protested. "No, of course not, Captain. But we cannot know who killed the Asiatic. We need time to think and choose the right moment to tell the general what we've found."

Bakaa drank some water, rinsed his mouth and spat it out. "It sounds reasonable, I admit. I was going to take the general to see the body for himself."

Ko replied a little too loudly. "No! Merseruka will recognize the mark and explode. If he accuses his men, the Setite assassin will become alarmed and escape. Let's allow him to think he is safe for now."

"You lowly toads are smarter than you look," Bakaa said. "Let's go."

They walked the short distance to the general's large pavilion. The old warrior was warming himself beside the fire outside.

"Good day, men," Merseruka greeted them.

"Not as good as we would have hoped, General," Bakaa said.

"Seth's rear end! What's happened? Out with it."

Bakaa said, "The prisoner's dead, my Lord. He killed himself."

Mereruka's face turned crimson. He walked inside his tent and returned with his sword. "Take me there, now."

Bakaa looked at the princes who could only roll their eyes. He led the general with Ko and Jet following behind.

Men of Ra Command greeted their general but he only grumbled unintelligible words as he passed them.

Upon reaching the place where the prisoner had been tied up, they found nothing.

"Well?" Merseruka bellowed. "Where is he?"

Bakaa's mouth hung open.

Ko said, "He was right here, General. We saw him earlier this morning. Sergeant Ibi showed us how he used a piece of sharp turquoise to cut his throat."

"Bring me the guards who were on watch with him all night," Merseruka ordered.

Bakaa obeyed and went to find them, returning with the two men. "Sergeant Ibi has disappeared, General. He's deserted."

"Gods!" the general bellowed. He moved toward the two guards, raised his sword, and in two sweeping strokes of the blade, cut off their heads.

Ko swallowed hard to keep from throwing up. He looked at Jet whose face in the sunlight had lost all its color.

The town of Pa-Osiris buzzed with activity. Two ships had docked and their passengers came ashore to meet family and friends. Cargo was unloaded, and the streets soon filled with people.

Semut parked his farm wagon in front of the general store. Sabu stayed with the horse, giving it bits of carrot.

When the king followed the farmer inside, he breathed in the wonderful mixture of spices—cumin, coriander, and cinnamon. Toasted nuts, salt, fresh garlic and thyme mixed with fragrances of various cosmetics on the counter. On the walls, samples of tunics for sale hung like trophies of some old battle victory. Hanging from the ceiling, other dried herbs added their scents to the large room.

Semut approached the owner with his list.

The proprietor greeted them. "Good day, Semut. Who is your friend?"

"I'm Alim," the king replied.

"Welcome, Alim. You're from Memphis?"

"Yes. We are taking a rest in your beautiful country. We love it here."

"Ah, then enjoy your visit."

The farmer handed the man a bolt of cloth he had picked up. "My wife will want four cubits of this, and the same with this yellow material."

After buying sacks of seed, the cloth, and a shovel, Semut settled his account. As they were about to leave the store, the king noticed a man enter and speak quietly to the store owner.

He thought nothing of it and helped the farmer carry their purchases out to the wagon. As Sabu helped them load, out of the corner of his eye, the king saw the owner and the man step out onto the wooden walkway in front. They were arguing and then the man started to walk way.

He stopped, turned back and shouted to the store owner, "I'm leaving on the ship docked at the wharf. It sails when the sun is directly overhead. You'd better be there before we leave."

The king saw something that suddenly caused him to drop a package he was handing to Sabu. His eyes followed the man as he turned and headed for the river.

A shiver ran down the king's spine and he had to grab onto the wagon to steady himself. He wasn't safe. Nor was his wife or Merry. On the back of the man's neck had been the mark of the god of darkness.

The Setites are everywhere. He gritted his teeth and swallowed hard. "Horus help us," he murmured.

13

In Zin, an irate general addressed his officers.

"How could Sargent Ibi, slip away from the two guards and carry the body away by himself?" Merseruka yelled at his six commanders. "You will find answers to this by the end of this day. Is that understood?"

The leaders of the six-thousand soldiers saluted and shouted with one voice, "Yes, General."

Merseruka waved them away, called for a beer and went inside his tent.

Ko waited patiently as Captain Bakaa spoke to the commanders. When he returned, he took the two princes aside.

"Seriously, Captain," Ko said, "How did he get beer in the desert?"

Bakaa said, "He has a private supply his aide keeps hidden. It's in a barrel that you would think had water in it."

"Gods, if his men knew about it, they'd mob him," Jet said. Changing his thought back to the problem he asked, "How long do we keep the discovery of the mark we found on the prisoner to ourselves?"

Ko said. "You know, if Jet's the target of these men, posting extra guards around us won't do any good if one of them is a follower of Set."

Bakaa sat on a large flat rock and pulled off his kaftan. "Perhaps Sargent Ibi buried the body in the sand so he wouldn't have to carry it."

"Un-unh," Ko said shaking his head. "The two guards would have stopped him."

"Not if he drugged their water," Jet said.

"It's no use talking about it. He's long gone by now," Bakaa said. "All we have to do is make sure the men who protect you don't have the mark. Will that relieve your worries, Highness?"

Jet said, "I hope so, Captain."

One of the general's aides hurried toward them out of breath. "Captain, the general has given the order for us to advance."

"Very good."

The aide saluted and left.

Putting his hands on the shoulders of the two young royals, Bakaa said, "Will you trust me to choose the ten men to guard you?"

Jet looked toward Ko who nodded.

"Good. Then I will begin my search." Bakaa turned and headed for the camp near the mining caves.

Not all was peaceful in Pa-Osiris. An anxious king stood by the wagon and pulled the farmer by the arm. "Hurry, Semut. Drive us out of town, now!"

Shocked that the king had touched him, the farmer, "What is it Alim?"

"Obey me. Get me out of here."

Babu, the king and Semut climbed into the wagon. With a flick of the reins, the horse pulled away from the store and headed back to the farm.

The king was too upset to talk on the way. He knew the farmer was confused, but he didn't say anything. When they reached the farm and stopped in front of the house, he climbed down and walked to the porch.

Semut and his son followed him. "What is wrong, Majesty? Please tell me."

The king lowered his voice. "That man back in the store. He was one of them. I saw the mark on his neck. We must leave here at once."

"No, Majesty. Please listen, I beg you. Did the man recognize you? Does anyone in town know who you are?"

The king shook his head. "No, he was arguing with the store owner."

"Great One," Semut said, "he may have wanted something delivered to his ship. I thought that's what I heard him say." He paused a moment. "You mustn't say anything to your family. There is no need to frighten them over this."

Color slowly returned to the king's face and he leaned against a post holding up the porch. "Maybe you are right. I would ask for soldiers from the garrison, but then everyone would know we are here."

"Good. For now, let's take the packages into the house."

Just then, Merry opened the door and walked toward them. "May I help?"

Semut said, "Carry the cloth to your mother, young farmhand."

She giggled and then ran her hand over the material. "Oh, they're beautiful." Picking them up, she carried them into the dining room.

Field workers had seen the wagon arrive and helped Sabu remove the sacks of seed. One of them untied the horse and led it toward the stable beside the barn.

The king sat on the edge of the divan in the front room. The joy he felt earlier in the day was gone. Fear once more crowded in and threatened to destroy his life. But the farmer was right. He couldn't frighten his wife and daughter. He did believe, however, that he needed someone to be his eyes and ears in town.

After the evening meal, everyone relaxed again on the porch. The wonderful fragrances of jasmine, freshly blooming lilies, and apricot blossoms filled the air. The king motioned for Semut and Sabu to walk with him into the garden.

"I have decided something, my friends. Semut, choose a farmhand you trust with your life to be our liaison in town. Perhaps he can work at the general store or the docks."

The farmer scratched his short beard. "Sabu and I have talked about this, Noble One. Horus must have inspired us. Nsu, one of the single men, could move into town. His aunt owns the only inn near the dock."

"Excellent. We will honor him for doing this."

"He must be told who you are and what we expect of him. Nsu is easy-going and will not share what he knows even when drunk. This I can swear to."

The king nodded. "Very well. I will tell him personally."

Semut said, "Tomorrow, I'll bring him to the house when the women bring us water at the first work-break."

"You and Sabu will be with us as well," the king added.

"Agreed." The famer nodded respectfully, turned and walked with the king back up to the porch.

The next morning, when the water clock's level was at the eighth hour, the women carried drinking water to the field workers.

Semut walked with them and called Nsu to follow him to the house.

"What is it, Semut? Have I done something wrong? You only call workers to the house when you dismiss them."

Semut laughed. "No, no. Don't worry."

The king was waiting with Sabu when he entered the front room.

Semut said, "Nsu, you know this man as Alim, but listen to me carefully when I tell you the truth. This is His Majesty King Djed. He is here for our help."

The young man didn't know how to react. His jaw dropped and he furrowed his brow.

The king said, "It is true, Nsu. I am Djed, King of Kemet, Son of Aha, Son of Horus-Ra."

Nsu fell face down trembling. He held his arms outstretched with his palms turned toward the king. "Have mercy Great King."

"Stand, Nsu. Your king is asking you for help."

The young field hand got up slowly and looked at Sabu and Semut who were nodding with reassurance.

"Sit with us, young man. You have my permission to do so. We have much to talk about."

Nsu sat down but couldn't stop trembling.

"Semut, will you tell him?" the king asked.

The farmer said, "Forgive him, Majesty. Allow him time to get over the shock."

"Of course. Take your time, Nsu."

Princess Merry entered just then, interrupting. "Sorry, Father." Then she saw Nsu. "What are you doing here?"

The king said, "He's going to help us, Merry. Leave us in peace."

Chastened, she bit her lower lip and left, walking toward the dining room.

Nsu began to shake his head. "No one is going to believe me."

"What will they not believe, my friend?" the king asked.

"That I taught the king how to pick corn."

Semut and Sabu burst out laughing, and the king joined in. "And I am grateful, Nsu. You were very kind to me. However, if you ever tell anyone, including your wife if you marry, I will have you entombed alive."

Nsu's smile vanished, and he stared down at the floor.

Semut said, "Here is what we are asking you to do. Leave the farm and move into your aunt's inn. Find a job in town—preferably at the docks. Some very bad people are after his majesty and his family. They are followers of Set, the dark god, and have his mark on the back of the neck."

The king studied Nsu closely. He was tall and had seen perhaps twenty summers. Rugged looking, he was well-muscled from working the fields. But his wide eyes and mouth hanging open, told him the young man was having trouble believing what they were telling him.

His majesty said, "What I say is true, Nsu. I saw such a man today. He had the mark of Set on him and that's why we hurried back to the farm."

"And what do I do if I see someone?"

"An excellent question. He must be arrested immediately," Semut said.

They were silent a moment to consider the answer.

It was Sabu who thought it. "Report it at once to the soldiers at the garrison. They will arrest him."

The king turned to Semut. "Do you know any of the soldiers?"

"I do," Nsu said. "Captain Rubi is in charge. He's honest, and has shown bravery when marauding ships from the Great Sea tried to rob the town. I know he loves the royal family, my Lord, especially your father—we remember his name." He bowed his head for a moment before continuing. Speaking softly he said, "I saw King Aha once when I was little. His ship stopped here. It was a great day for all of us."

His majesty nodded. "We must bring the captain here, Semut."

"Yes, and must be told what is at stake," Babu said.

"Arrange it at once. Now, can you move into the inn today?"

The young man nodded. "Yes, Majesty, if my aunt has a room."

"Tell her we will pay for your room, even if she has to move someone out."

"What reason do I tell everyone I'm leaving the farm?" Nsu asked.

The farmer said, "Tell them I ended your employment. Make up a reason that sounds plausible."

The king became even more serious. "Remember, my name is Alim. Don't let 'majesty' or any other royal expression escape your lips, Nsu, or we will all die."

Nsu swallowed hard. "I understand." He turned to the farmer and added, "You see, Semut. I was right. You did bring me to the house to let me go."

In the arid land, far north of Kemet, the Army prepared their advance.

"I'm not getting up on that thing," Ko insisted. "They smell and spit at you."

Bakaa said, "The general has ordered us to try them. We took over one hundred of the beasts left after the battle. If Asiatics can ride them, so can we."

Ko said, "I'll try if Jet does."

"What are they called anyway," Jet asked.

"The desert people call them gamal," Bakaa answered. "Can you believe that the word comes for their word for beauty? Getting on one is easy and you control them a lot like a horse with your heels and a small whip."

Ko walked toward one already saddled. It was kneeling down and he climbed up. The animal didn't budge, but just sat there. "Why isn't it moving?"

"Shout at it and kick your heels into its sides," the captain said.

Jet climbed up onto his animal and waited.

Ko held on tight as first the hindquarters rose up and then the front legs.

"Heeyaah, Heeyaah," Jet shouted as his beast suddenly snorted, rose and galloped away.

Ko did the same and his beast followed the other. He felt the thrill of being so high up and riding an ugly beast that actually had grace and strength as it moved across the sand.

Jet yelled, "I didn't ask how to stop it."

Ko kicked his beast's sides and pulled back hard on the reins. "Stop," he yelled and pulled hard again. The animal slowed and then came to a halt. "Down," he shouted.

Jet was finally able to turn his mount around and brought it to a stop close to Ko. I'll take a horse any day."

"Me too, but I do admit these creatures are good at a gallop."

They waited for Bakaa and the others to catch up on foot and then gave their desert beasts to other men who quickly climbed up, eager to try the strange desert animals.

"What did you think?" Bakaa asked. "Should we take some of them back with us to Kemet?"

"Why, Captain?" Ko answered. "We don't need them. We have boats and ships to take us wherever we want. Most of us live close to the river. We can't use them."

"Except in the desert," one of Bakaa's men said.

Ko grinned. "But who wants to live in the desert, soldier?"

"Good question," Bakaa said.

The army entered a narrow pass bordered on each side by granite hills pushing up from the sands. They resembled small mountains reaching for the sky.

"This would be a great place for an ambush," the general said when he caught up. "Be vigilant. Pass the word."

An even colder wind blew in from the north, but diminished as the sun set behind the western formations of stone hills.

The warriors built fires with dried acacia branches and thorny cactus. As dusk faded into the blackness of night, an eerie wailing began on the tops of the range of hills around them.

Behind them, a hot wind from Zin rushed toward them, causing many of the men to remove their kaftans so they could sleep on them.

"There it is again," Ko said. "Can you hear it, Jet? What is it?"

"I don't know. The cries are almost human—yet they're too deep and menacing."

The voices increased and no one could sleep. Covering their ears didn't help.

"These hills don't want us here," Captain Bakaa said.

"What do you mean?" Jet asked.

"It is said that the gods use the winds to carry out their will."

He had no sooner said it, than a cold strong northerly wind met the heat of the southerly one from Zin and began to spin in the middle of camp. Blankets flew up into the night sky. The wind became so strong, Ko had to stab the ground with his short sword and hold on to it like a ship's anchor in a storm. He used his other hand to protect his eyes.

"The wind gods are angry," a soldier shouted and another repeated his cry until the whole army was shouting with fear. And then, the winds abruptly stopped and the unearthly cries were gone.

As they relit their fires, someone noticed a shape moving high on top of the cliff. "Who's that?" someone shouted, "There's a man up there."

Ko turned his face up and saw a dark figure raising his hands and pointing them toward the army below.

The apparition shouted in a loud voice, "The gods of the winds defy you. Go back sons of Kemet before it is too late."

His words echoed through the narrow pass

Another figure appeared on the cliffs, but closer to camp. "Hear me, abhorrent dwellers of the river. Our gods will not let you pass."

A loud murmur began in the ranks and passed through the army like a slow moving roll of thunder.

General Merseruka's loud voice made his men turn toward him. "Warriors of the Great Djed, Son of Aha. The gods of Kemet are with us. It is only the wind."

He had barely spoken when a blinding flash of lighting lit up the sky. The thunderclap that followed shook the ground so violently it knocked men to the ground. Many covered their ears and fell face down in fear.

Jet mumbled to Ko, "I would say the gods of the desert winds have sent a clear warning."

14

As the all-powerful Ra brushed aside the morning mist, Merseruka's soldiers didn't want to get up. Most had not slept at all because of the wind and haunting cries in the night.

"General," someone called.

Merseruka said, "Approach."

"I must report dead soldiers. Thirty of them, maybe more."

The general's pavilion, badly torn by the winds, offered little protection. He stood in the makeshift opening and scowled. "What caused it? Were we attacked?"

"No, my Lord. One blast by the bolt of light from the night sky destroyed them. We must leave here. The desert gods will send more winds to destroy us."

"Gods, gods? I am sick of gods," Merseruka shouted.

"Please, General," Captain Bakaa said. "Do not anger the gods further, I beg you."

"You're right of course. I do not wish to offend them." He paused, "Signal the trumpet to play the advance."

Bakaa sent a man through camp to give the trumpeter the order.

When the trumpet call went out, their counterparts in all of the battalions repeated the call several hundred times. The soldiers marched wearily forward.

After a long, long time, the seemingly endless desert began to change. Low ridges rose naked from the sand and grew into a mountain range of which nothing remained but the barren rock.

The princes and their newly assigned ten guards stayed close to the general.

Bakaa asked, "Where are we heading, General?"

"To the tallest mountain, Captain. The desert people say it is holy, and the home of their gods. It's not far."

"Is it wise to provoke more anger from them, my Lord?"

"No, Bakaa, it's not the gods we seek, but the gold. That's why his majesty has sent us north into the land of the Asiatics. On the mountain, more gold than in all Nubia is hidden deep in the ground—or so they say."

Ko didn't like what he was hearing. He said in a low voice to Jet, "If gold is the blood of the gods, and the general is going to steal it, how can the gods not respond?"

As if to answer, a blast of cold air forced everyone to pull their hoods up over their heads. The wind blew thin and dry. Dust rose around their feet.

On the farm, the king stood at the front door of the farm house watching a rider approach. He stepped back and waited for the man to come to the door.

Semut hurried forward to let him in.

"Is there a problem, Semut?" the officer asked.

"Come in, Captain Rubi. There is someone here I want you to meet."

Queen Nakhneith and Princess Merneith entered the room and stood behind the king.

King Djed took a step forward. "I am the son of King Aha, and this is your Queen and Princess."

The captain grinned and turned to Semut. "What kind of pleasantry is this? Did you call me all the way out here for your amusement?"

"Please, Captain," Semut began.

The king raised his voice. "If you leave here, it will be our death, Captain. Do you recognize this ring?" He held up his right hand bearing the ring that bore his majesty's throne name.

"Just a moment—let me see it." Rubi read the king's name and suddenly his eyebrows rose in shock and his knees trembled.

"Here is more proof, Captain," the king said. His wife and daughter pulled back their hair exposing the royal seal on their necks."

The officer fell face down, and then knelt on one knee. Thumping his fist to his chest, he said, "Forgive, Majesty. How could I know?"

The queen and princess sat on the large divan.

The king continued, "This is very important, Captain. Your men must not find out that we have sent Nsu to live at the inn, at least not yet. He is looking for members of the followers of Set. They are everywhere and want to destroy the royal family. If Nsu sees one, as we did yesterday, you will arrest him immediately. Tell him the king has issued an order that these men are to be hunted down and killed."

Captain Rubi rubbed his chin. "Of course I will help, Majesty. I thought they were all destroyed years ago. I remember when they killed your mother the queen in the temple of Horus." He paused and bowed his head for a moment. "We honor her name. Yes, I remember them well."

"Good. We too thought them all destroyed. My uncle, General Akhom, killed them if you remember. But somehow, like a persistent disease, these evil demons have returned."

"Does Nsu know you've told me all this?"

"Yes, Captain. I pray no other follower shows up here, but now we will be ready. Horus go with you."

The captain knelt again and saluted. Then, nodding to Semut and Sabu, left the house.

In town, Captain Rubi sat at a table in the inn drinking a jar of beer. The room smelled of unwashed customers, onions and sour wine. A warm loaf of flat bread waited to be broken in half. He took some of the honey on the table and covered the piece he'd taken. He recognized Nsu at once when he came down the stairs. The two made eye contact for a split second and Nsu left the inn's dining room.

A large fleshy woman approached his table. "We don't see you in here often, Rubi. As owner, I know everyone in this small town."

"My feet were killing me, Imi. I ducked in here to cool them off."

The woman laughed. "Now that's an honest reason to come in. The next beer is on me."

Rubi nodded and raised his cup to her.

Taking his time, he finished his bread as he glanced around the room. He tried to see a mark on the backs of other people's necks, but found it more difficult than anticipated. People's hair usually covered their ears and necks. He would have to get much closer to spot it.

Nsu was waiting for him when he left the inn.

"I'm glad you finally came out, Rubi."

"Captain Rubi to you. We were not to be together. What is it you want?"

"I've found one," Nsu said.

"What?"

"I've found the man with one of the marks."

The Army of the North continued its march through the Valley of the Moon. Their advance was easier than anticipated. There was not as much sand as the Zin, but they found mostly dry river beds with smooth rock slate. It made it easy for the few horses they had to walk on.

Only one half of the general's pavilion was usable. His barrel of beer, smashed in the windstorm put him in a foul mood.

At mid-morning of the second week, a scout rode into camp. "It's there all right—the mountain of the gods. It is two days ahead, General."

The men cheered and their voices reached the next battalion who repeated the jubilant cry.

The scout dismounted and approached the general. "One of my men was killed, General. A good man. An arrow struck him down. On the shaft was this message." He handed Merseruka the small piece of papyrus.

"Set's foul stench!" the general cursed. He handed the note to Bakaa who shared it with the princes. They read the words together:

"The Crown Prince will die high above the earth."

The symbol of Set was on the bottom.

Jet looked at Ko and then walked away. When Bakaa made as if to follow him, Ko said, "Let him be. He'll work through this on his own. It's just the way he is."

Bakaa nodded and went back to the general.

Later, when Jet returned and sat by Ko's fire, he wouldn't talk. His cousin knew to let him be alone. He would speak when he was ready.

Archers had bagged several quail and shared them. Ko roasted one on a spit and when it was done, offered half to his cousin.

"I'm grateful," Jet said. "But wouldn't you really be glad for some fish about now?"

Ko chuckled. "Yes, I really could enjoy a fat river perch."

Jet took a bite of his quail and said, "Did you understand that message?"

"Yes and no. I think the 'high above the earth' refers to the sacred mountain, don't you? That's where they will try to kill you."

"Why? It doesn't make sense. Why bring us all the way out here to kill me on our search for gold? Is that what they want? The gold or my life?"

"They probably believe they can have both, Cousin."

"What can I do?"

"I've been thinking about it and have a plan, but you must agree to it."

"Very well, explain."

Outside the inn in Pa-Osiris, Captain Rubi asked, "Where did you see him?"

"He's back in the same store Semut said he was in several days ago. My boss at the shipping office sent me to the store for a jar of honey, and I saw him in there. He may still be there."

"Did he know you'd seen him?"

"No. Why would he be interested in me anyway?"

"Are there any others you've seen at the docks with the mark?"

"No, only him, but of course I'm not allowed to go aboard the ships."

"I'll meet you at the store. Go on ahead."

Nsu headed for the general store and went inside.

The captain wasn't far behind and slipped inside by the back way. Walking around the store, he glanced at the shelves and turned so he could watch the man at the counter. Moving toward him, Rubi said, "I see you've just come ashore, stranger. Are you traveling on the Phoenician vessel?"

The man turned and Rubi saw the small brand behind the ear.

"Yes, I am. Is there a problem?"

"No, not that I'm aware of. May I see your papers?"

"They are in my cabin on the ship, Officer. I'll come with you if you like and we can get them."

"Very well. I'll wait until you are done here."

"I'm finished. I'll come now."

Rubi saw Nsu leave. The young man knew what to do. They had worked it out. He would hurry to the garrison and call for four soldiers to help the captain make an arrest. As Rubi and the man left the store, they walked through town toward the river. Four soldiers met them, grabbed the man who tried to struggle and knocked him out.

"Lock him up but two of you stay with him at all time."

"Yes, Captain," the biggest of the four guards answered.

They lifted their prisoner and carried him toward the garrison.

Rubi turned to Nsu. "Well done for a farmer."

"Let's hope he's the only one, Captain," Nsu replied.

As the princes approached the general, Jet asked, "What if we meet another Asiatic army, General?"

"Then we fight. We may not have their ugly beasts, but we outnumber them."

"We're with you, my Lord. May I also ask who informed you about the mountain?"

Merseruka rode awhile in silence.

Jet thought maybe he was debating whether to tell them or not.

"It was old chamberlain Ankhkahf. Remember him? Maybe you were too little. He served under your grandfather and father. He will have seen eighty summers by now. He found a map of the mountain made by an early expedition to Ta Maf Kat."

"You mean he knew for sure there was gold there?"

The general nodded. "Well, they didn't find any, but the desert people told him where to look. Before they could dig, a war broke out with the Asiatics and our men were forced to leave."

It was Ko's turn to ride awhile in silence. Finally, he said, "So this campaign is to find the gold. Is that it?"

The general turned in his saddle and leaned a little toward the young man. "No, of course not, Highness. There's plenty of gold in upper Nubia. We've known that for ages. The king, your uncle, wanted us to clear the way to the city of Byblos on the Great Sea. It is where they build the best and fastest ships. We are to capture the town for him. Kemet would then control the Sea Peoples. From there we will sail home by way of the Great Sea and our sacred river."

The Crown Prince rode up to join them as Ko asked his last question. Jet asked, "If this is a mountain of the desert gods, don't we risk a curse for disturbing the sacred places, General?"

"You have fear because of the message, Highness."

"Yes, General, only because it is my name on the papyrus."

"I will personally take you to the top of the mountain. And I will show you there is nothing to fear from these desert gods. Can they withstand Horus or the great Ra? Do they have the power to raise and lower a river? Have they made their desert tribes wealthy and well fed?"

Jet smiled at the general who returned it. "It is a comfort to know you are willing to risk your life for us, General. Ko and I already have a plan when we reach the mountain."

"That's more like it, my Lords," Merseruka enthused.

On the farm, the royal family prepared to enjoy their evening meal. Everything was ready, but before they could sit down, an insistent knocking on the front door demanded attention.

Semut walked into the living room and opened the door. It was Nsu.

"Sorry to disturb you, Semut."

"What are you doing here? I thought it was agreed you would stay in town."

"Yes, yes, I know. But I thought you'd like to know we arrested the man we saw in the shop a few days ago."

"Ah, that is good news indeed. Come in and tell Alim."

Nsu followed him into the dining room, and the young man didn't know what he should do, bow, or fall prostrate, so he simply nodded his head.

"Nsu has good news," Semut said.

"We heard," the king said. He stood and patted the young man on the shoulder. "This is good news indeed. Where is he now?"

"In jail, Sir. Captain Rubi's men have him on constant watch."

Semut's wife said, "Well, thank goodness that is over. Why not invite Nsu to join us at the table, Husband?"

"Yes," the king said. "An excellent idea. Join us my boy."

Semut kept an eye on his former farmhand to make sure his country manners did not upset or offend his royal guests.

The princess asked him about his new job in town and Nsu told her.

Another loud knocking made everyone stop eating.

Semut hurried to the door, exasperated at the interruptions. He yanked it open only to find Captain Rubi standing there.

"What is it, Captain?

"May I step in? I have some bad news."

Semut's heart skipped a beat. "We are at the table. Can it wait?"

"No. The king must be told."

"Come out onto the porch. Tell me there," Semut said.

Outside in a softer voice, Rubi said, "The Setite is dead. He took poison in his cell. We couldn't revive him."

15

When the king heard the word "dead," he rushed out onto the porch.

Captain Rubi saluted. "Forgive us, Majesty. The prisoner killed himself. He too poison hidden on his person."

The king's face contorted in anger. "May he rest in Seth's abyss and suffer the fate of the cursed. I may consider such a fate for those who failed to search the prisoner too."

Rubi's face reddened. "Majesty, to really be safe, I should inspect all passengers and crew on ships now docked."

"We agree," his majesty said, slipping into the royal 'we.' "We would also recommend you and your men patrol the town at night. I fear now, we cannot keep this from the people any longer if we are to catch these devils of darkness."

Rubi lowered his voice but wouldn't look at the king. "Forgive me for presuming, Great King, but I think you should send for the royal galley at once to take your family home. You have Royal Guardsmen to protect you. We can't do that here. You were safe in Pa-Osiris until we discovered this man. Please consider it."

"You are right, Captain. Can I trust you to send a messenger pigeon to old Ankhkahf at the palace? He will know what to do. He and I talked about this possibility." The king paused and looked the younger man in the eyes. "Forgive me for saying it, but we've seen you have no mark on you. We ask you to return with us to Memphis. We are confident you would protect our family with your life."

"I would, Majesty," Nsu said. "It will be an honor to travel back with you. I lost my wife and daughter last year to the coughing sickness. There is no one to hold me here."

"I feel better," the king said. "Now, make sure you are the one to write the message for the pigeon yourself. Put the name of the old chamberlain on the outside—not mine. Include these words: 'the man with the broken tooth' orders it. He will know it is from me."

"Yes, Majesty, I will go at once."

The king and the others watched the young officer climb onto his horse and ride off.

Sabu said, "I hate to say this, Majesty, but you will take one of our best residents with you to Memphis."

"I agree," Semut said with genuine regret in his voice. "And I will miss you, Majesty. I think you would have made a good farmer."

The king smiled. "I could not have asked for a better compliment. My Nakhtneith and I will remember this farm all our days. We will honor you for what you have done."

When the message from Memphis arrived, the king read it and said, "Ah, it is his handwriting alright. His hand trembles these days, but there is no question it is his. He then read aloud:

To him with the broken tooth,
May the gods bless you.
The old man with the broken toe
Sends an affectionate greeting.
The message is received and the

Wind of Shu is sailing today.

The servants of Horus are ready.

Merry frowned. "That is an unusual message, Father. I did not understand all of it. A broken tooth, broken toe? What is that about?"

The queen laughed. "It is our secret language with the old chamberlain, Merry. We use phrases that only our family would know. For example, 'He with the broken tooth' is you father. As a little boy, he ran after his father once, tripped on a stone and fell, breaking his front tooth. He cried for ages."

"I see," the princess said. "No one would know that but Father and the chamberlain."

"Yes," the king said. 'The old man with the broken toe,' is the chamberlain of course. Recently, during the visit of the ambassador from the Sea Peoples, Lord Ankhkahf slipped on the polished floor and fell on his noble behind. The fall also broke his left foot. We never let him live it down."

The queen smiled. "It is good to know our galley is coming for us. I will be glad to go home again, but sad to leave this family. I have learned so much about our people and their lives. Perhaps it will make us better rulers, now, Husband."

"I too have felt the same regret about leaving, Beloved."

Sabu said, "I hope this means I can get back with my unit in the army."

"We will have to see, my boy," the king said. "I am certain the army will be glad to have you back."

Rubi said, "Permit me, Great One, but there is still a problem. How do we get you to the ship without being mobbed? The whole town will discover you are here when they see your ship."

"When will it arrive?" the king asked.

"I would assume it will anchor off shore and dock in the morning, Majesty," Rubi answered.

It was Sabu who suggested a solution. "Semut can drive you into town, Majesty. People will think nothing of it. You won't stop to talk. Instead, he'll take you directly to the ship where your guards will escort you on board."

"It's too simple," Rubi said. "It will not work."

"Why not?" the queen asked. "People who have come to the farm to buy food, have not recognized us. This will be no different."

The king nodded. "She is right, Captain. We must not have your guards around us. We will simply act like we are back in town to buy more supplies."

The princess said, "Since Nsu works on the docks, why not have him watch for the ship's sails and ride here to tell us when it has arrived."

The king put his arm around her. "Clever girl. You know, one day you will make some prince a wonderful queen."

"I know, Father. I've already picked him out."

"Oh? Really? Who is it?"

"Mother knows, but she is sworn by the gods not to tell."

The king laughed. "So there is a conspiracy in my own house. I will not have it." He stomped around the room like an enraged fool, making everyone laugh. Zee, the cat, however, was so frightened she jumped up into Merry's arms.

When they settled down, the king eased himself into the farmer's big old chair with cushions. "I am going to miss this chair."

"And I will miss the goats and ducks," Merry said. "I have also loved learning how to sew with mother and Rabiah."

Her father said, "I will not only miss this old chair, but also the openness people have with each other here in the country. There is no strict protocol telling us who can speak when and with whom. There is pleasure working beside another man in the fields and being able to sweat without someone rushing around me trying to wipe it off."

Semut said, "Think what we too have learned, Majesty. "Unlike most people, we have experienced how real and kind the royal family is. We normally only see you royals as polished granite statues—far removed from our lives. But now, we know that kings and queens are living persons—blessed by the gods to rule our lives and live amongst us. We always knew that you were not be spoken to, touched, or looked upon—royal laws that are very important. But during these days on our farm, we know differently. Your father, King Aha, Majesty, would be very proud of what you have become."

Strangely moved by the farmer's words, the king took a deep breath. The farmer's words were not to flatter, or gain anything. They came from the man's heart. He nodded to the man who smiled back.

Before going to bed, the royal family packed what little they had into leather bags, and placed them in the front room.

As the sun answered the summons of the rooster chorus, everyone ate a morning meal of eggs, fruit and goat cheese.

Nsu and Babu arrived and ran into the house. "It's here!" they shouted. "It's nearing the town but has anchored some distance from the port."

When the wagon was loaded, the king rode up front next to Semut. Sabu, the women, and cat, sat in the back with the bags. The journey into town was uneventful. People along the way waved to them and they waved back.

When the wagon reached the dock, Semut turned the wagon so the king and family could more easily get out and walk up the gangway.

Out on the river, the Wind of Shu raised anchor, furled the sail, and under the power of one-hundred oarsmen, headed for shore.

Rubi had ridden ahead to tell his guards to keep the curious onlookers away from the wagon and the gangway.

As the ship turned to align itself with the dock, the crew threw ropes ashore to make it secure. Royal guardsmen rushed down the gangway and knelt in salute to the king.

"Where is our Captain of the Guard?" the king asked.

"Bakaa is with the Army of the North, Majesty." One of the guardsmen answered.

"Of course, I'd forgotten." The king stepped down and Captain Rubi reached out to steady the king's arm.

An officer struck Rubi and two guards held him down.

"Stop," the king shouted. "This is Captain Rubi of the garrison here in town. He is our guest."

"But Majesty, he touched the royal person and must die."

The king frowned. "If I fell overboard would you refuse to save me Captain? Where is your reasoning?"

"Forgive me, Majesty," the man fell face down on the ground.

Rubi and Sabu helped carry the baggage aboard. The royal family followed them on deck. When the crew saw their majesties, they face down on the deck until the king raised his arm for them to carry on.

"Captain," the king addressed Rubi, "tell Semut and his wife to wait a moment, and bring me my small leather bag."

Rubi nodded and went to the royal cabin and returned with the bag and handed it to his majesty.

He then went down the gangway and asked the farmer and his wife to follow him back on deck.

A large crowd gathered, curious to see if the king was on the galley.

His majesty decided to enter the cabin and changed into the royal garments put there by his servants in Memphis. When he walked back out on deck, he walked to the railing and responded to the crowd's cheering by waving to them.

He then walked back and met Semut and his wife. Taking them to the far side of the ship, they would be able to talk privately.

"I have called you on board to express my appreciation in a more tangible way. I had to wait for my ship to bring it." He reached in his bag and said, "Semut, hold out your hands, palms up."

The farmer did so, and the king poured dozens of gold coins into his hands.

"Oh, Majesty," the farmer's wife exclaimed.

"I want you to buy a pair of horses to help on the farm," the king said.

"Great One," Semut said, too moved to speak. He finally whispered, "Just knowing you and your family was reward enough. Thank you for such a generous gift."

"Hide the coins before you return to the wagon. May the blessing of Horus go with you and protect you."

Rubi carefully studied the guards around the king. His eyes fell on the captain of the guard who met them on shore. When the man suddenly moved too closely to the king, Rubi rushed forward and shouted, "Majesty, step back!"

Alarmed, the king backed up immediately.

Rubi pulled the dagger from his belt and thrust it into the heart of the officer.

The guards rushed toward Rubi but the king raised his hand. "Stay back."

"What was it, Rubi?" the king asked.

"Look, Great One. There, behind the man's ear."

Six thousand soldiers stared at the enormous mountain on the horizon beckoning them.

"There it is," the general declared. He reined in his horse and dismounted. "We will camp here tonight."

Ko marveled at how long such a simple command from the general would take to reach the last soldier. When the dust settled, the prince's ten guardians fed the horses.

His cousin nodded toward the mountain. "It's higher than I thought it would be."

"Will you climb it with me to prove their gods cannot defy ours?" Jet asked.

"Of course. I cannot let you have all the gold, now can I?"

Their personal guards built a fire and settled down close to the royals.

"Our shadows are beginning to annoy me," Jet said.

"Why? They are here to protect us. You cannot resent them. We need them."

"Of course, we do, but it does not mean I have to like them. All they talk about among themselves is their weapons and pray for another war with the Asiatics. Of yes, and they never bathe, so be sure to ride up-wind."

One of the general's aides appeared as if from under a rock. "He's calling for you both, Highnesses."

"Is he serving us our evening meal?" Jet asked in his best sarcastic tone.

Frowning, the aide shook his head.

When they arrived at the general's tent, Ko said, "We are here, General."

Inside, the veteran soldier held up several old maps and placed them on a small table. "Approach," he said. "I want to show you where the gold is hidden."

The young men leaned over the map showing the drawing of a subterranean cave.

"If it is so easy to find, how could there be any gold left, General?" Jet asked.

"Everyone is afraid to go near it. The mountain is sacred and forbidden for anyone to touch it. They say people and animals are struck dead when they try to walk upon it."

"Fear is a good way of keeping gold-seekers away," Ko said.

The general took a deep breath. "If you look closely, Highness, there is also a cavity near the top. I would imagine that could also be where the blood of the gods may be hiding."

"Then I will have to go find out," Jet said.

The general shook his head. "No, Prince, I forbid it. Have you forgotten the warning? It said you would die high above the earth."

"Ko is coming with me and of course my ten guardians."

"I cannot concur, Prince. I was charged by your father to protect you on this campaign."

"Then come with us, General," Ko suggested.

"What? No," the older man said, genuinely surprised by the idea.

"We need to study these trails," Jet insisted, running his finger along one side of the map of the mountain. He sat on a folding stool and leaned over the table. "Here is where the trail up the mountain begins."

As they examined the map, a loud shout from thousands of soldiers reached them.

Ko ran outside followed by the others. At first, standing there in the murky dusk, everything suddenly became still. Then, the mountain trembled and the ground under their feet shook. A deep red glow crowned the summit. Bright yellow streaks spread out from the top and deepened to oranges and reds.

"It would appear the gods of the desert have come home," Ko said.

On his majesty's ship, Captain Rubi led the queen and her daughter to the royal cabins. A few minutes later, the king walked in and hugged Merry and his wife. "I'm glad you didn't see what happened, my loves."

Captain Rubi had stationed himself outside their door.

The king opened it and called him inside. "You saved our lives, Captain. That man could have killed us, and the gods only know how many guards are loyal to him."

The captain said, "We'll have to check them out individually, Great Kemet."

"I agree. But how may we reward you for what you have done, my friend?"

"Let me be part of the Royal Guards, Majesty. I can think of no higher honor."

"Done as of this moment. The queen is a witness. Now call in that evil captain's aide."

Rubi went out and called for the men to bring the next in command of the guards."

When the king saw him, he said, "Ah, Sergeant Teti, thank the gods it is you." He motioned for the sergeant to stand. "This is very important, so listen carefully. I want every guardsman and crewman examined for the mark of Set. Anyone you find, arrest them, and tell Captain Rubi. I have promoted him to Captain of the Guard."

"Understood Majesty. We didn't really know the officer Captain Rubi killed. We didn't understand why he took Captain Bakaa's place. No one imagined he was part of the Set brotherhood."

Rubi shook his head. "How could you not see the mark on him? You worked with him every day, and washed together."

"It was not obvious to us, Captain. With his nemes head covering, we couldn't have seen the mark. None of us would have thought an officer could be disloyal to the king."

The king said, "Captain Rubi, call Manu, the ship's captain."

Rubi saluted, went to the door and ordered one of the crewmen to bring the captain at once. When sergeant Teti came out, he said, "Be very thorough in your search, Sergeant."

"Of course, Captain."

———————————

As Sergeant Teti made his way down the steps to the crew's quarters, he rubbed his neck behind his ear. He checked his finger to see if the thin skin-colored paste he used to cover the mark was still there. Pleased with himself, he began his search.

16

Captain Manu had sailed royal galleys since the time of Aha, the king's father. He watched king Djed grow not only in the knowledge of what it would mean to be king, but what it meant to be a man. He liked him and would do anything for him.

On the other hand, he didn't like Teti, Sergeant of the Guards. He and the now dead Captain always kept to themselves, and didn't fit in with the other men.

"I'd keep my eye on that one," Manu told Rubi, pointing to the sergeant as he came up the steps from the hold.

Rubi said, "You will be pleased to know, Manu, that all of your crew including yourself have passed inspection."

"What about the Guards?" The captain asked.

"I'm nearly finished and haven't found the mark on any of them. But I do find it hard to believe that the officer I killed was the leader of this tight group of men."

"He wasn't, Captain. He came on board at the last moment. However, the transfer had all the official seals on them."

"Seals can be copied. And it doesn't sound reasonable he would be put in charge of the Guards accompanying the king." Rubi paused and then added, "I've spoken with all the men, and none of them knew anything about the man—where he came from, or where he trained. What are the odds of that?" He leaned on the railing and studied the riverbank moving past. "I'm not overly religious," Rubi continued, but I believe Horus had something to do with me saving his majesty just now. Only the Divine Protector of the Throne could have prompted the king to choose me to return with him. Nothing can explain it. Yet I felt compelled to come with him."

Manu nodded. "I agree. The gods did this, Captain." His voice reverberated with mystery.

Rubi asked, "Other than the king, who is responsible for the oversight of the Royal Guards?"

"One of the generals of the army, Captain. I don't know which one."

"I see. Well, the king told me that General Merseruka is in the north fighting the Asiatics, and the Crown Prince is with him. That leaves only General Intef leading the Army of the South. I will speak with him when we reach Memphis."

Manu said, "You have an important role in protecting the king, Captain. You will need the courage and wisdom of the gods."

Rubi gave the older man a brief salute as Manu nodded and returned to the helm.

Darkness still reigned in the faraway land of the mountain. Prince Ko had fallen asleep stretched out on the ground with a good view of the plain. The nickering of the horses woke him, and he found the earthquakes had diminished. He stood and stretched his sixteen-summer old frame, and worked on the kinks in his neck. Abruptly, another earth shock made the horses whinny and cry out.

Darkness fled the promise of sunrise as Jet walked over and stared at the mountain in the distance. "What kind of magic lives in it?"

"It's not magic, Cousin, although we can see now why the desert people believe their gods live there. I've heard of these kinds of mountains. The people who live around the Great Sea call them 'mountains of fire.'

"But this one has no fire, Ko."

"I know, at least not that we can see from here. That's what I find mysterious."

General Merseruka wandered toward them and stood scratching the back of his head. "I know one thing, young princes. After last night, I will not go up that mountain with you."

"I've changed my mind, too, General," Jet said. "How could anyone in their right mind consider climbing it? It shakes the earth and spews out red and yellow light."

The general nodded. "I couldn't sleep all night. That mountain lit up the sky the whole time. The ground trembled so much it knocked over tables and chairs and broke the tent poles."

"What do we do now, my Lord?" Ko asked.

"We go forward. Our ultimate goal is Byblos, but we will give the mountain a wide berth."

"A wise decision, my Lord," Jet said upending his waterskin and gulping down the precious liquid.

Captain Bakaa hurried toward them. "Bad news, General. "One of those flashes of light killed over forty of our men—burned to black cinders, all of them." He paused before continuing. "I hate to say this, my Lord, but I believe the gods sent the fire down on us. They do not want us to cross this desert. We must turn back."

"Control yourself, Captain," the general growled. "People pass this way all the time—desert people, and trade caravans."

"But you didn't see those men burned to ashes, General. Nothing on earth could have burned them like that."

Merseruka said, "I understand. The gods rule in the heavens—the winds, the clouds, the sun and moon. But there are forces even our wisest men do not understand—the power of the land and sky themselves."

"You are our General, my Lord. We obey your orders," Bakaa said.

"Sound the advance, Captain. That is my command."

Bakaa saluted and walked away.

Ko looked at Jet and shrugged slightly. The blast of the first trumpet sounded and the camp came to life. The general's aides packed up what was left of his pavilion and loaded it into a wagon. Each warrior rolled up his blanket and tied it onto his back along with a water skin. Because of the morning chill, most chose to wear their kaftans.

As Ko saddled his horse, he couldn't help thinking about the gold. When his cousin rode up alongside, he said, "You know, Jet, if we leave without finding the gold, your father might need it in the future. We may be losing a great treasure."

"You make a valid point, Cousin."

"I meant no disrespect to the king, but his resources come from the gold of Nubia. What if Nubian gold runs out? Maybe we could take back a huge supply for your family's treasury?"

"Oh, no, Ko. I see what you are trying to do. You only want to get me up that mountain so the assassins can kill me."

"Will you be serious, Jet. We have to consider the gold, don't we?"

The Crown Prince rode awhile without responding. Ko thought he may have pushed him too far.

"Let me think about it," he finally said as they headed down a ravine toward more level ground.

Ko smiled. They might get the chance to climb the mountain after all.

The Wind of Shu, with the royal family aboard, arrived at the capital in the afternoon of the next day. When Rubi made his report to the king, it pleased his majesty they could not find any other followers of Set.

Crowds of well-wishers lined the docks as the galley settled into its accustomed berth. Carrying chairs for the royal family awaited to take them home.

A contingent of fifty warriors would march on each side of them along the boulevard to the palace.

The royal family emerged on deck in their royal attire. Servants placed their clothing on board when the ship sailed from Memphis to bring them home. Cheers echoed off the buildings as their subjects welcomed them home.

The queen and princess left the ship first, escorted to their chairs by the new captain of the guard. Her majesty wore a long pleated turquoise gown, and when the gentle wind touched it, it surrounded her like a blue-green mist.

Princess Merry chose a pure white robe that reached to her knees. She carried her cat in a basket of reeds covered in gold bands to hold it together.

Captain Rubi assisted each of them to their carrying chairs, and returned to stand behind the king.

His majesty looked straight ahead but spoke loud enough for Rubi to hear. "I have learned that the kings in cities around the Great Sea, ride in vehicles with two wheels, pulled by horses."

Rubi said, "I heard they are dangerous, Majesty." He stepped forward and followed the king down the walkway.

His majesty wore the gold crown of his father. Gold necklaces of his ancestors covered his bare chest.

Rubi stood beside him as he mounted his white stallion brought to the ship by the guards. The magnificent horse pranced and stomped its front legs in recognition of its master.

Overwhelmed by the size of the crowds along the way, Rubi wondered how he could protect the royal family from so many. He looked suspiciously at every person who threw flowers on their path.

His responsibilities ended when the royals reached the palace. Servants rushed out to escort the family inside.

"This way, Captain," Sergeant Teti said. "I'll show you to your command post."

From habit, Rubi glanced at the right ear of his aide but could find no mark of any kind.

It only took the new Captain of the Guard a short time to settle into his small office. A door connected to his bed chamber, a much smaller room. As he sat with his feet up, he decided to begin something he had thought about doing on the ship.

He called into the hallway, "Sergeant Teti. Bring all of the guards to me one at a time."

"Yes, Captain," Teti saluted and walked off.

When each man entered, Rubi asked about his training, family and how long he had served at the palace. He then explained the danger to the royal family from the followers of Set and made each man show him the back of his neck.

By the end of the afternoon Teti said, "That's all of them, Captain."

"No, it's not, Sergeant. Have a seat."

When he finished with Teti, Rubi couldn't find anything in the man's background or training which was out of the ordinary. Still, a nagging suspicion about the man continued to bother him. He could replace him, of course, but there had to be a good reason.

The next day, while walking through the long corridors of the palace, Rubi happened to glance into the king's garden and drew in a sharp breath. Teti sat with the princess at a small pool. They laughed and Merry splashed water at her cat.

Rubi walked toward them and when the sergeant saw him, he stood to attention.

"Where are the four guards who are assigned to protect her Highness?" Rubi demanded.

The princess said, "Oh, Captain. I did not want to have those four big men following me around everywhere. I thought one guard would do."

Rubi nodded. "Sergeant, wait for me at the garden entrance."

Teti frowned, but turned and left.

Rubi asked, "What is the name of your cat again, my Lady? I have forgotten."

"This is Zeezee, Captain. Her real name is Aziza, 'the precious one.'"

The beautiful feline walked over and rubbed her cheek against Rubi's shins. He bent down and stroked her back, provoking a loud purr.

"She wants you to sit here by the pool with us," Merry said.

"I'm on duty, Princess. I don't think I. . . "

"Nonsense, Captain. Captain Bakaa used to join us, why can't you?"

Rubi gave in and sat on the raised stone edge of the pool. Zeezee jumped up onto his lap.

"See, she likes you. But she's been naughty today."

"Oh, what has she done, Highness?"

"When the Sergeant picked her up, she scratched him on the neck. Bad cat," Merry scolded, shaking her finger at her.

"Why didn't she scratch me, I wonder?"

"Because you are nice, Captain. She can tell that about people."

The cat jumped down and sat on the edge of the water staring at a small gold-colored fish swimming back and forth.

"She's going to catch that fish one day," Rubi said.

"I hope not, Father gave it to me as a present last year."

Rubi stood. "I really must get back to my post, Princess. It was nice meeting Zeezee."

Rubi sensed the girl wanted to say something more and he waited patiently.

"You know, Captain, how we were all upset by the mark you found on the other captain's neck—near his right ear?"

"Yes, my Lady."

"I think you should check the Sergeant's neck. When he wiped the little bit of blood the cat's scratch left on his neck, some color came off on his hand and I thought I saw something dark behind his ear."

Rubi's heart beat faster. "Thank you, Princess. I'll make sure it isn't the mark we are looking for. You have a sharp eye, for a woman that is."

Merry punched him on the arm and laughed. "Be gone you wicked man."

Rubi walked inside and headed for his office. Normally his aide should be there when Rubi left. Instead, only the guard on duty stood watch.

"Where has the Sergeant gone?" Rubi asked.

"I don't know, Captain."

"The king," Rubi whispered heading for the king's apartments. He hoped he could get there before the sergeant. Convinced now the man was an agent of the brotherhood, he blamed himself for not finding it before. At the ornate golden doors of the king's residence, the four guards outside stood in place.

"Where's the sergeant?" Rubi asked.

"Inside, Captain," one of the guards answered. "He said he had a message from you for the king. The Queen has joined them."

"Open the doors," Rubi ordered. He then rushed into the foyer and the steward came toward him. "Where is his Majesty?"

"On the veranda with the Queen, Captain," the steward said.

Unsure of the layout of the apartments, Rubi finally saw the open doors leading outside. To his horror, Sergeant Teti stood next to the king showing him a parchment scroll.

Running forward, Rubi shouted, "Watch out!"

Teti pulled a dagger from his belt and raised it to stab the king when Rubi's body struck him, knocking him down. He grabbed the sergeant's wrist with the dagger and bent it so it cracked. Rubi pulled out his own dagger and thrust it into the man's heart. Blood spurted out, covering Rubi's chest.

"Gods!" the king shouted.

The queen screamed and hurried away.

Rubi stood, grabbed a cup of wine from the king's table and splashed it on the neck of the sergeant. Using a piece torn from his kilt, he rubbed the man's neck and a flesh-colored paste used to hide the mark, came off.

"Look, Majesty," he said pointing to the man's neck.

The king moved closer and saw the mark. He then walked into the front room and collapsed on his easy chair. "Come inside, Rubi."

The captain walked in and stood there with blood running down his chest, and onto his torn kilt.

The king's breath came in short gasps. "That's twice you've saved me, my friend. I should make you a general."

The queen entered the room with a servant who carried a towel and basin. "Clean up the Captain," she ordered.

As the servant washed him, Rubi smiled when he saw the chair the king sat in. "Ah, Majesty. I see now why you liked that old chair in Semut's farmhouse. But yours is of much better wood I venture."

His words made the king smile. He ordered the servant to bring more wine for them and the officer. "You may sit in our presence, Captain. Her majesty and I are grateful once again for your intervention. The gods have blessed you with keen eyesight and bravery."

"Not I, Great One. Princess Merry deserves the credit this time."

"Merry?" The queen repeated. "How could she have seen or known that horrible man?"

"Well, maybe it was her cat who deserves the credit, Majesty."

The king's eyebrows went up. "Zeezee? How could she be involved?"

"I'll explain, Mighty Picker of Corn."

That made the king laugh again.

"Her cat scratched the man on the neck and your daughter thought she saw the mark of Set when the coloring he had put on it rubbed off on his hand."

"I cannot believe it. Saved by a cat!"

The servant arrived with the wine, and for a few moments, they sat and enjoyed a refreshing breeze wafting in from the river.

Two guards slipped in and removed the body of the dead sergeant far from the royal presence.

17

Bivouacked north of the desert of Zin, General Merseruka addressed his officers:

"Horus Company will advance toward the mountain." He turned to Captain Bakaa. "It is only fitting that the king's Company find the gold."

"And the king's son can make the claim, General," Prince Ako said.

"Indeed."

"Who is going to tell him?" Captain Bakaa asked.

"I am in command," the general said.

Ko nodded. "Then, as a good soldier, Jet must obey."

Bakaa smiled. "With his Highness, things do not always go as planned."

Ko laughed. "You know him well."

Bakaa said, "According to the old maps, the earlier expedition believed the gold is buried on the west side of the mountain—the side facing us now."

Ko folded his arms. "I do not know much about mining gold, General, but it will certainly not be lying there on the ground waiting for us."

"One of our wagons has picks and shovels, Highness. We will use them to see what is there. If the gods are kind, and we find what the desert people call the blood of the gods, we will leave one of our Companies here to guard the mine."

Ko's eyebrows shot up. "But how can a thousand men survive out here?"

Merseruka said, "We will supply them from the Great Sea north of here. We will defeat the Sea Peoples on our way to the ocean. With them under our control, we will be able to bring in regular supplies to our men."

Prince Jet rode toward them. "When will we reach the mountain, General?

"Tomorrow, about this time, Highness."

"Why are the other companies heading northwest? By the position of the stars last night, I noticed they were moving to the other side of the Great Mountain."

"You reason well, my Prince. Horus Company is going on ahead to see if the earlier expedition that found the gold was correct."

"Last night there were no earthquakes or colorful displays," Jet said. "Maybe it is over." "While it is calm, we can search for the caves," Bakaa said.

"Let us ride on ahead, Cousin," Jet proposed.

"All right, we do have ten shadows with us, remember."

"Of course. There is no going anywhere without them."

"Heeyahh," Jet yelled, kicking his heels into the horse's flanks. The stallion reared up and broke into a gallop. Ko followed close behind.

Taken by surprise, their bodyguards ran for their horses, and raced after them.

As the sun climbed to its highest point, the men of Horus Company finally reached the foot of the mountain of the gods. Surprisingly, they found a large oasis with fresh water. A spring flowed out of the side of the granite mountain. The young princes abandoned their clothes and jumped into the large pool, splashing and playing like children.

Later, when stretched out on a large granite slab, Ko said, "This is almost as good as being near our sacred river. I will not worry about Horus Company now. Where there is water, there will be animals."

"Do you still have the map to the gold?" Jet asked.

"Yes. Why?"

"I think we should first ride around the base of the mountain. Perhaps we can do it in a day."

"Perhaps, Cousin, but this is the biggest mountain I have ever seen."

Captain Bakaa walked toward them. "Well, I see my two river frogs have found their element. Put on some clothes. I want to show you something."

The young men pulled on their kilts as the captain led them into the underbrush. "Break off one of the leaves of this spongy plant. Go on. . .do it."

They obeyed and Ko said, "Now what?"

Rub the exposed end of the leaf onto your skin. The sap will protect you from the sun's rays. Smear it on faces, legs, arms, everywhere. Wear it for the day, and wash it off in water at night if you can."

"It is not bad," Jet said. "There is no smell."

"We have decided to go for a ride, Captain," Ko said. "Tell our ten shadows to mount up."

"Where are you headed?"

"Around the base of the mountain. We want to look for the caves."

"I'll tell the guards," Bakaa said.

Protected from the sun, the princes fed their horses, led them to water, and then saddled up.

"Which way should we go?" Jet asked.

"I think we should go north and then follow it around," Ko replied.

"Lead on," Jet said, reining in his horse. "Where are our guards?"

"They will catch up. Come on."

The young men let their horses canter, taking the time to study the base of the mountain for any unusual shapes or openings. They hadn't gone far when without warning, a spear flew toward them, followed by another.

"Down," Ko shouted.

Jet threw his leg over his saddle and leapt from his mount.

They drew their short swords and crouched behind a large boulder.

Another spear struck the boulder and bounced off.

The hoof beats of the ten guardians signaled they'd arrived. They drew their arrows and fired toward the underbrush when the next spears where thrown. Cries from the hidden attackers enabled the men to advance on the unseen enemy, releasing arrows as they charged.

Ko shouted, "Take one of them alive. That's an order."

It didn't take long for the skirmish to end. The tallest guard, and obvious leader of the ten, dismounted and walked toward the crown prince.

"Are you all right, Highness?"

"Yes, we are unharmed," Jet replied.

"Oh, and I'm well too, Soldier," Ko growled. "How are you called?"

"I am Soris, Highness. I meant no insult."

"Who are these people, Soris?" Jet asked.

"Desert people, Noble One. We killed a dozen of them and captured one."

"This is bad," Ko swore. "It was not wise of us to bring down the wrath of these people on us. They know these places like their own skin"

"You said to one, Highness," Soris said. "That was your order."

"Very well, blame me if you will, but I say we will regret what we have done this day. It is a mistake."

One of the other guards brought the prisoner forward. He pushed the darker-skinned man onto the ground in front of them. "I know one of our men speaks their tongue my Lord. Shall I bring him?"

"Do so," Jet said. "We will wait here. Bring more waterskins as well."

The guard saluted, and leaving the bound man to Soris, climbed onto his horse and hurried off.

Ko studied the prisoner. He wore a much lighter-weight kaftan, was barefoot and had a short black beard.

Soris searched him and pulled out a dagger, three knives, and a curved sword from the man's clothing.

Startled, Soris said, "Look at this, Highness. I have never seen such a weapon. It would be deadly in hand-to-hand combat."

Jet marveled. "He is well armed indeed. Were they all so equipped?"

"Yes, Highness. And something else. There were no women or children with them. They were a hunting party and we found two antelopes, plenty of quail and a few hares. Our men will be glad for them."

"A hunting party," Ko said, mulling it over. "That means there must be a settlement nearby. Thanks the gods there were no families with them."

Soris frowned. "Why would we care, Highness?"

Jet growled. "That kind of thinking, soldier, makes me fearful of our march toward Byblos. His majesty, the Great Djed would not approve killing women and children."

"Wait, aren't we all killers, Highness?" Soris asked. "A warrior who is ruled by sentiment can't be the warrior he needs to be."

"Enough," Ko said. "The riders return."

Two men rode toward them, and the man behind the first, jumped down and knelt on one knee and saluted the princes.

"Your name?" Jet asked.

"I am Nuben, Great Son of our king."

Ko said, "Ask the prisoner who he is and why he attacked us?"

Nuben faced the prisoner and asked the questions. At first, the man refused to speak, but when Soris pulled out his sword, he answered.

Ko liked the pleasant musical quality of the desert man's tongue. Almost a song, but with a single-noted chant.

Nuben said, "He says, Highness, that he is one of the Bedayi, or Bedouin. Their men attacked us because we have invaded their land. Everything here belongs to them—animals, plants, water—all of it. The gods of the desert winds gave it to them before the moon was born."

Ko nodded. "Tie him up tighter and give us a horse. I want him and you to travel with us around the base of the mountain. We will come back here later."

"Why?" Soris asked.

Jet scowled. "If you want to continue in your role as pampered guard, Soris, you will cease these questions. I am not pleased."

Ko smiled as the strong, imposing guard swallowed his response. Instead, he simply nodded and stood at attention.

Turning to Nuben, Ko said, "Ask him how we should honor his dead hunters."

Nuben did so. "They leave their dead out on the sand, Highness. They must dry naturally in the sun and rejoin the elements as the gods will it."

"Not very civilized is it?" Jet said

"Should we allow him to do what he says?" Ko asked.

Nuben said, "I think we should take care of the bodies when we return, Highness. We can ask the prisoner to show us how it is done."

Ko shrugged. "I agree. Now let us gather up their weapons, mount up and continue our search around the base of the mountain."

As they saddled up, Nuben pulled the prisoner into the saddle behind him.

"Take care he doesn't choke you, Nuben," Soris warned.

Ko rode toward their ten guardians. "We are grateful for saving us from the ambush. You will be rewarded when His majesty hears of this. We have long memories."

His words pleased the men and they mounted up, turning their horses around to follow the royals.

"I beg forgiveness," Soris said. "One of us should ride up front. There could be more Bedayi up ahead."

Jet nodded. "Agreed. Our lives are in your hands."

The royals and their guards carefully made their way along the base of the mountain. They stopped at several other springs to drink, and allow the horses to rest. When they started again, Ko saw an abnormality perhaps ten cubits above the base. A dark crevice cast a shadow across the mountainside. He reined in his horse and tied it to a small palm. He started to climb over boulders that had fallen from earthquakes.

Jet followed him with the guards scrambling behind.

"Wait, Highness" Nuben shouted. "The prisoner says not to go up there. Many have died."

"Bring him up," Ko ordered.

The prisoner struggled and tried to resist until two guards picked him up by the arms and carried him to the princes.

The desert man jabbered on and on and Ko could see the fear in his eyes. He bit Numen's arm when he tried to calm him, and then yelled something at the top of his lungs. It was a cry Numen couldn't translate.

Suddenly, he stopped and faced the two young princes.

"He says, Highness, that this is an evil place."

Jet looked at the man, but something on the ground caught his attention. "Move him away," he ordered. On the ground was what looked like a smooth stone.

Ko bent over and picked it up.

"Gold," Jet exclaimed "This has to be the place."

The guards picked up some of the gold and examined it under the bright sunlight.

"What I thought might have been a shadow, is really an opening," Ko said. He pointed to the cave above them in the mountainside. "It must be at least twenty feet tall."

"I can't believe it. There could be a great treasure inside," Jet said.

"We need a torch," Ko suggested. "What can we do?"

"I have my flint," one of the guards offered.

Using a dried acacia tree branch, the guards wrapped some palm cloth from a dwarf one growing in a crag of the mountain. Then, using cord from a guard's saddlebag, they tied up the prisoner, and wrapped the rest around the branch.

Striking the flint against a piece of granite, over and over, they finally built a small fire and used it to light the torch.

Soris said, "Let me go first, Highness." He drew his sword and carried the torch in front of him. "There could be cobras in here, scorpions, who knows what else. Watch your step."

"I see something ahead," Jet said. "Up there at the edge of the cave something is reflecting the light."

Ko followed, trying to watch his step in the dim light of the torch. "You are going too fast," he complained.

Unfortunately, the ground shook and everyone lost their balance.

"Gods" Jet swore. "Not while we are in here. Horus, protect us."

As if in response, the ground stopped moving.

Dusting themselves off, the four of them moved deeper into the dark recesses of the cave.

"Here it is," Soris said.

Jet stood beside him. "Unbelievable! There it is—the wall of gold."

Ko moved closer as his cousin ran his hand over the dusty wall, and gold shone through—glimmering in the light of the torch.

"This is where the general's men can use picks and shovels," Jet said, the torchlight revealing his broad grin.

They turned and started back, but abruptly, the anguished cries of the other guards outside, reached them. Ko rushed to the entrance and saw spears thrown from above the opening in the mountain.

"The hunters are killing our guardians," Ko shouted back to Soris and the prince.

Soris shouted, "The prisoner's getting away." He rushed out and was struck by a spear that ran him through. The mountain shook again—causing a large boulder to fall and land at the entrance to the cave. Rocks of all sizes rained down on the entrance, blocking their exit.

"Help," Ko shouted, but almost choked on all the dust inside.

Jet shouted, "Don't leave us here."

The mountain shook again causing more boulders to fall, sealing up the entrance completely. A small opening let in some light, and Ko saw someone moving outside.

"Help," Jet shouted. "Get us out. We can make you very rich."

There was no reply. Instead, the shadowy shape placed a rock in the opening, sealing their doom.

A deadly silence filled the cave. They continued coughing as dust settled on them. The torch still burned, but would soon die out.

Jet coughed up more dust, but finally managed to breathe. He said, "That message the followers of Set sent me, was wrong, Ko. Remember, it said I would die high above the earth, not a hole in the side of the mountain."

Ko was too frightened to respond as he watched the small flame of the torch flicker and go out. He reached out a grabbed his cousin's hand. "Horus help us," he whispered.

18

"No!" Akhom shouted, tossing and turning in bed.

Something had awakened Ko's father in the middle of the night. Whatever it was didn't feel right. He pulled on his kilt and walked out onto the veranda of his house next to the palace. Still strong and physically fit, he had survived forty summers.

His wife followed him outside and put her arm around him. "Tell me, Husband."

He turned and embraced her. "I didn't want to wake you, 'Frini. I'm sorry."

Princess Nafrini's long black hair brushed against his bare chest and he pulled her closer. "Tell me, please," she repeated.

"It's Ko. Something's happened to him."

Nafrini gasped. "Not Ko," she whispered and collapsed onto one of the divans on the veranda. "Have the gods taken him?"

"I cannot tell, beloved. But it troubles me. It could mean Prince Djet faces trouble as well." He walked to the railing and stared at the great river sparkling in the moonlight. "I can't tell his majesty yet. I will pray for the gods to reveal it to me."

"Ah, then you must go to Asheru, the king's seer. Let him help you find out what the gods are trying to tell you."

"You are beautiful and wise as ever, Nafrini. Jet and I are lost without you."

"Go, wake the seer. He won't mind. He knows it will bring him more money."

Akhom, trusted advisor to the king and his nephew, went back into their bedchamber, put on his golden sandals, and picked up a dark-blue linen wrap. The nights were cool, and he kissed his wife before leaving the house.

The seer lived not far from the royal complex of houses and apartments. Close enough to the king's palace when he needed them. Still not comfortable with magic having power over his life, Akhom walked begrudgingly to the seer's home.

A stray dog barked at him as he walked through the old priest's garden, he ignored it, and it ran off. He tapped on the wooden door, but there was no answer. Knocking more insistently, a light was lit, and a servant came to the door, rubbing the sleep from his eyes.

"Lord Akhom, come in and sit. I will awaken the master."

In the light of the small oil lamp, Akhom glanced at the charts and images of the stars and horoscopes on the walls. A few torn ones hung by a seemingly magic thread. The pungent fragrance of incense permeated the room causing him to cough and clear his throat. Troubled by second thoughts about being there, he nodded as Lord Asheru came into the room.

"Lord Prince. You honor us with your presence— and at such an unusual hour."

"Apologies, Lord Priest. I could not sleep. Something awakened me, and my wife insisted I come to you."

The elderly man smiled. "The gods chose a wise woman for you. Let us sit in my consultation room and you can tell me everything."

Akhom followed the elderly man who smelled of sweat and perhaps too much wine, taking a chair across the table from the former priest.

246 ~ William G. Collins

"I have a question, my Lord. Does my son live or not? He and the Crown Prince are in the northern desert."

"Ah, as far away as that," the old man mumbled. "Let me fetch the scrolls of the two princes and the stars." Walking to another room, he returned with a rolled-up papyrus. "We have the exact time and date of Prince Ko's birth and his cousin Jet's as well." He called his servant to bring him a cup of wine, and when it arrived, he took out powder from a box on a nearby stand and mixed it into the cup. "This will clear my head and allow me to discern the truth."

Akhom frowned, convinced the old man had taken a drug.

Asheru reached in his box again and brought out several flat ivory pieces with detailed images painted on them. Worn by use, he now placed them in a stack. He chose one, which when turned over, showed a red star. He drew in a quick breath. "I holed the great red wandering star, my Lord, known as the eye of Set."

Akhom grimaced when he heard the name—Set, killer of kings and their families.

"The red star signifies conflict and uncertainty, confusion and war, sadness and misfortune and in the end, violent death."

Akhom swallowed hard and clenched his jaw.

"Ask your question again, my Lord."

"Is my son alive?"

The seer swayed back and forth on his chair, his eyes closed. He mumbled and Akhom could tell it was some kind of incantation—but no sound came from his mouth. Then, he became very still. "I hear the sound of breathing. There is darkness all around."

"Yes, yes, go on."

"Wait, there is another sound. . .someone else is breathing. . . two are breathing. They live my Lord," the magician collapsed.

Akhom stood and walked around to make sure the seer still breathed and opened the door.

The servant entered. "The master must rest now, my Lord."

Akhom nodded and gave the servant a silver coin.

As the prince walked home in the dark, the full moon sank behind sand dunes in the west. Akhom took his time, and somewhere, a rooster crowed. While receiving a positive answer to his question about his son, he still felt uneasy about the gods awakening him when they did.

"The gods want to tell me something," he mumbled.

At home, Nafrini breathed a sigh of relief at his news. "Did he make you feel better?"

Akhom shook his head and sat on his favorite chair in the front room, kicked off his sandals and a servant rushed in to wash the dust from his feet.

"How can I put my trust in magic and ivory images, my Love? We know that *Ma-at*, the perfect balance of our Kas, comes from the gods. There is nothing we can do to change what they will."

Nafrini frowned. "I won't debate this. Asheru's answer gives me comfort. Let me get you a lemon-grass tea to help clear your head."

Akhom nodded and leaned back in the chair. "His majesty loves these country chairs he discovered while on the farm. Practical and comfortable. I'm going to ask the carpenter to make me another."

A light tapping at the front door prompted the servant to answer. He hurried to the front room and said, "Master, the king asks for you."

"Oh? At this hour? Tell the messenger I am on my way."

The servant went back to the door but returned immediately. "The guard says he must wait until you accompany him, my Lord."

"Then it must be serious." Akhom put on his sandals, hurriedly drank his tea, picked up a piece of bread and ate it as he walked toward the door.

The guard led the prince along the private path that servants and staff used to reach the palace. Inside, the guard said, "You know the way, Highness."

"Of course."

When he reached the private apartment of the royal family, the door stood open and King Djed waited with his fists on his hips. "What took you so long, Uncle?"

"I will ignore that remark, Majesty, considering I used to change your *shendyt* when you were a baby." He walked past the king into the front room.

"I could have you flogged for that remark."

"True, but first, why did you call me, Nephew?"

The king looked around to make sure they were alone. "Something has happened to my son."

Akhom's eyes grew bigger. "Have you had a troubling dream, Majesty?"

"No, I simple woke up with a sense of foreboding. Something happened to them, Akhom."

The older man leaned forward in his chair. His voice softened. "I have had the same foreboding, Majesty. I felt this way once before on that hunt in the marshes with your father—we remember his sacred name. Then, the message from the gods came too late for me to help him. I regret it to this day."

The two men were silent a moment before Akhom continued. "I had only just returned from Asheru's house when your guard came to my door."

"Ah, what did the old sorcerer say? I'm not sure I trust him in these matters."

Akhom nodded. "Exactly. After consulting my son's charts and drinking a magic potion he says that my son lives. The old man said he heard two persons breathing in a dark place. I pray it was Jet and Ko, and they're still alive, Majesty."

"The land of *Taf-kat* is so far away, Uncle. No messenger pigeons will cross the desert, and we can't send a ship to Byblos. It would take too long to reach the army."

At that moment, the door to the apartment opened. The Queen Mother, Lady Khenthap entered. Dressed in a long white robe, her hair was in disarray, the creases from her bed's pillows still lined her cheeks. She resembled a ghost. "I knew I would find you awake, my Son. You couldn't sleep either?"

The king walked to his mother and embraced her. "Come sit with us, *Me-wet*," he said.

"Tell her, Akhom," Djed said.

Akhom began with his astonishing foreboding that awakened him, certain that something had happened to Ko. And now after his visit to the seer he had just learned of the king's similar premonition.

"We must listen to the gods," she said. "I saw the two of them as well in a kind of dark room. They were by themselves, and the earth shook. Abruptly, spears flew toward them. It frightened me. I feel we should go to Horus and pray for their safety."

"I agree," Akhom said, standing and moving next to the Queen Mother.

The king walked into his bedchamber and returned wearing a clean kilt and several gold necklaces across his chest.

When they were about to leave the apartment, the king said, "You know what the magicians say about the number three. It is an evil sign. And here we are—*three* of us: Akhom, Mother and Me. I pray this number is not a bad omen."

At the foot of the great mountain, General Merseruka growled, "What do you mean the princes haven't returned? They only went for a ride."

Captain Bakaa said, "But they did not come back, Lord General."

"Saddle my horse. If they've gone off on their own, I will kill them both with my bare hands."

Just then, a rider raced into camp. "Sir, we found nine bodies of desert men staked in the sand not far away."

"Desert men? What do you mean?"

"Local hunters, General. They have our arrows in them."

"Impossible," Bakaa said.

"Take us there," Merseruka ordered.

When they reached the place, they found the nine dead hunters, completely unclothed, staked down in the sand. Small bits of feathers and plants decorated the bodies as if in observance of some ritual.

"The arrows are ours, all right," the soldier said, pointing to one of the dead men.

"Captain," the general said, "have we had any reports of contacts with desert dwellers?"

"None, General. I don't know how this could have happened."

"Yes, well, let's begin our search around the foot of the mountain. That is where the princes and their guardsmen were going to start."

Merseruka mounted his horse again and followed the captain toward the base of the mountain.

"I'll send for our best scout to help us follow their tracks," Bakaa said.

"Do so at once."

When the man arrived, he studied the imprints in the sand. "They've gone north, General. Follow me."

After a short distance, the scout stopped. "The tracks show a skirmish here, my Lord. You can see the hoof prints of their horses, and there are our arrows on the ground over there."

Bakaa said, "The hunters must have attacked our men, General. Perhaps our guards killed them in the ambush and moved on. But who staked them to the sand?"

Merseruka scratched his chest. "This is no time for questions, lead on."

The scout jumped back onto his horse and continued in the same direction.

After a long ride, they stopped at another spring.

"More tracks here, General. I count thirteen different horse tracks."

"Thirteen?" Bakaa said. "Are you sure?"

"Yes, Captain. They each have distinctive prints."

"But with the ten guards and two princes, where did the other horse come from?" Bakaa asked.

The sun had reached its zenith by the time they found another small spring. The men filled their waterskins again and allowed their horses to drink.

As they rode ahead once more, the scout returned out of breath. "They've killed our ten guards, General! Their bodies are up ahead. There is no sign of the princes."

"Gods! Those motherless sons of Set," Merseruka swore.

"Maybe they've taken the princes prisoner," Bakaa said. "Only the gods know what these jackals did with them. They might stake them out of the sand, too, while still alive."

"Enough, Bakaa. We know nothing. We'll wait here while you ride back and bring more men to help in the search."

The dark cavern had filled with dust and debris.

"I can't breathe," Jet said.

Ko wiped sweat from his forehead to keep it out of his eyes. "Come over here, Cousin. This gap in the stones lets in light and some fresh air."

"I always thought my tomb would be more glorious than this, poor brother toad."

"No one says this is your tomb, Jet. We can still hope they find us."

"How? We're sealed in with so many boulders, there's no way out."

"You always see the bad in things, Royal Gadfly. Horus will help us. I still believe the gods want you as king, and therefore, as your lowly cousin, he will save me too."

"Dream on." Jet said. "Let me near the opening." He stretched his neck, so his face could be as close to the space in the rocks as possible. He sucked in the air but also some dust which made him cough again.

"Wait," Ko said. "I hear movement outside."

"In here," they both shouted. "Come closer."

"Those are horses' hoof beats," Ko said. "They're looking for us."

The clanging of a sword on stone made them shout louder. Then the small stone that let in a little light began to move.

"That's it," Ko shouted. "Over here."

To the princes, it took forever for the soldiers to move it, but it finally flipped over backward. They could hear it bouncing down the side of the mountain.

"We've found them," a soldier shouted.

"Gods be praised," Bakaa's familiar voice reached them.

More metal blades working on the stones dislodged another stone and the young men could see two faces.

"Gods, you ugly toads!" Bakaa shouted. "You said you were going to ride around the mountain not dig inside it!"

"Get us out, Bakaa, I command you," Jet yelled.

"You have to come out here and make me do it, Prince," the captain growled.

"B-a-k-a-a-a-a. . .!" Jet shouted.

The captain smiled as he used his sword to help dislodge another small boulder. He whispered, "That's the spirit, Highness. Don't give up."

19

It took hundreds of the general's men and horses to move only three boulders from in front of the cave. The men passed food and water through a small opening to the princes.

One night, when Jet and Ko tried to sleep, the cave began to vibrate. The pulsating of the floor made the young men grab on to each other. The earth then shook so violently, the large boulders blocking the entrance fell away. Cool air rushed in and the princes gasped with relief.

Ko shouted, "It's open, let's get out of here."

When the guards who were on duty discovered them, they cheered and gave them a ride back to the oasis. They ate and then swam to get rid of all the dust, and ate some more, before falling asleep exhausted. They slept through an entire day and night.

The day after, they rode back to the cave and into the desert where ten mounds of stones covered the bodies of their bodyguards.

Prince Ko stood with the Crown Prince as the men of their Company honored the sacrifice of their friends.

"I'm sorry I treated our shadows so badly," Jet said to his cousin. "Especially Soris their leader."

"They died in their service protecting you," Ko reminded him. "Theirs was a noble death."

"Death is not noble, Ko. We must live for the here and now. Life today is what is important."

Afterward, they rode to a place in the desert where the bodies of the nine desert assassins lay, now blackened cinders. They were set on fire by Horus Company in revenge for their comrade's deaths. The general insisted their ashes remain exposed. Those desert dwellers he was sure were watching, would understand the army would not tolerate any more attacks."

"They will not have a place in the afterlife," Prince Djet declared. "May the gods of the underworld crush their Kas."

They then rode back to the cave to see the progress made in clearing the entrance. The men had managed to move more boulders with horses and ropes. With no hardwood trees available to cut down and make levers, it was going to take a long time.

Later, when they dismounted at the oasis, Jet asked the general," When will the men dig for gold?"

"It will be a long process, Highness. We will have to send men to bring more horses, wagons and tools to chip away at the stone. I am leaving a thousand men here, all of whom are fine archers. They should be able to survive on the game around the mountain."

"Are we ready to follow the army north, General?" Ko asked.

The general said. "We leave in two days, my young friends. But isn't there something you've forgotten?"

Jet shook his head. "No. I don't believe so."

"You were going to defy the followers of Set by climbing to the top of the mountain, Highness."

"Ah, the message from the Setites. Yes, I'd forgotten with all that's happened. After our entombment in the cave, staying alive became more important to me. I've had second thoughts about going to the summit."

260 ~ William G. Collins

"But the men heard you, Lord Prince," Merseruka said. "It was as if you made a vow to the desert gods to defy Set and his followers. You will let the god of darkness win?"

Ko frowned. The general was being unkind, provoking the prince and he didn't like it. "Why risk the Crown Prince, General?"

"If I remember, Lord Prince, you too were willing to climb with him. Am I wrong?"

"No, General. But I will do whatever the prince decides."

"Let me think on it another day, General. But if my memory serves me, you too agreed to climb the mountain. But when you felt the ground shake and the mysterious lights flash before you, you changed your mind."

The general cleared his throat. "Yes, well, that is right. What I will say is that I will do whatever you do, young Lords."

As the veteran officer moved off, Jet glanced at Ko and they nodded, satisfied the general would go with them.

They tied up their horses and walked toward the men preparing their food.

Ko asked, "Why risk the climb, Jet? Let's just march north with the army and take a ship home."

"I want to prove to the men and to myself, that I will not be swayed by superstitious curses from Setites. They haunted my grandfather to his death. I will not have them around during my reign, Cousin.

We should have killed them all back then when we had the chance. Your father would have led the effort, but my father wanted the land to heal after King Aha's death. I understand now that was a mistake."

That evening, the two royals stretched out on blankets beside the oasis pool.

Ko watched a wild duck paddling on the water, but something wasn't right. Ripples appeared on the surface, but there wasn't any wind or breeze. The ripples became more frequent, and then the earth trembled, gently at first, but grew in intensity.

A strong hot wind blew in from the desert. It bent the palms almost to their limit.

One of the men suddenly shouted," What is that?" He pointed to the top of the mountain.

Ko leaned back on his blanket and saw great clouds of smoke rising near the summit.

"Is it smoke or a water mist?" Jet asked.

A violent tremor dislodged a large section of the mountainside which came crashing down, narrowly missing the army's camp.

Earth shocks continued until dark. High above the frightened warriors, bright white and yellow flashes rose to the heavens. And then, a sudden cold wind blew down from above. It picked up blankets and anything not secured.

Jet said, "Where is our god Shu—god of the wind? Surely he is more powerful than all of these desert gods?"

He spoke quietly, causing Ko to smile. His cousin was afraid of upsetting Shu or any other gods.

Ko backed up to the trunk of a tall palm, Jet stood beside him. "What about those superstitions now, Cousin? The gods of the desert winds are unhappy with us. The general should give the order in the morning to retreat from this place."

The wind blew out their fires. As a last resort, the men curled up in their blankets and prayed the night would end.

The moon rose in the east and as its rays touched the mountain, they calmed it—no rocks fell nor ground shook. However, a strange and eerie sound emanated from above them.

"It is coming from the mountain and sounds like singing," Ko said. "That's not possible."

"Since when do mountains sing, Cousin?" Jet grumbled.

"Well, you explain it."

Captain Bakaa joined them. "It is the wind, royal tadpoles. Shrubs growing on the mountain have long thorns on their branches. They are so thin the wind blowing through them makes music. Much like when we play the flute or the lute. The wind becomes the fingers, plucking those thorns making them vibrate—thus the music."

"That stretches belief, Captain. Have you heard this before?" Jet asked.

"Yes, in the delta, Highness. When there is a storm on the Great Sea, some of the reeds growing on the riverbanks snap and the wind rushes through their hollow stems, making similar music."

"Well, that is a relief," Ko said. "It gives credence to the myth about the mountain. The gods of the desert winds do live on the mountain and protect it."

"Myths are for children," Bakaa murmured.

"I don't know, Captain. When we were entombed in that cave entrance, we heard strange sounds that neither Ko nor I could explain."

The officer shrugged. "Well, Highness, our wise men tell us there are always explanations for everything."

"Easy explanations?" Jet said. "Then what is the easy explanation for why you are the ugliest military instructor we have ever had?"

Ko burst out laughing. "Now you are in for it."

Bakaa joined in. "There is no explanation, my pompous toads. My father is even uglier than I am. So, there you are. It is in our blood."

"Sad," Jet said. "And to think, if you have a son, he will be even uglier."

"Enough," Ko said. "Are you going to come with us in the morning, Captain?"

"No, I choose to stay here on solid ground. I think this is a bad time to go, with the mountain expressing its displeasure on us being here."

"You speak as if the mountain is alive," Jet said.

"What would you call it, Highness? It breathes, through the winds we have felt tonight. It sings, as witnessed by the music made by its servants, the winds. It moves, causing the ground to move in all directions. It smokes, sending billowing clouds up into the heavens. Yes, I am convinced it is alive—in its own way."

"Now, with that, I'm going to try to sleep," Ko said, stretching out again on his blanket.

Early the next morning, General Merseruka awakened the two young men. "Ra's glory is here, young masters. The mountain is quiet, and we have a long way to go."

Ko yawned, stood and stretched first his legs and then his arms. "Good morning, Lord General. Do we know the way? What about guards to protect us?"

"One of our scouts showed me a shepherd's path winding up the mountain. All we must do is follow it. Of course, he didn't go all the way up, but explored it for me so I could lead us today. We will not need guards, Highness. It will only be us three. No one is going to attack us."

Jet joined them, rubbing his eyes, and drinking handfuls of water from the pool. "I'm ready. Lead on, General."

Merseruka grunted and started up the rocky path with the two men behind him. It followed a zig zagging configuration which made ascending easier. The hardest part of the climb was enduring the heat from the glaring sun. In addition to rubbing the sap from the plant on their skin, they also wore their kaftans to shield them from its rays.

By mid-morning, they were more than half-way to the top.

"I can barely see the summit," Ko said.

The general said, "I need to rest a moment." He sat on a flat rock and drank from his waterskin.

When they continued, the sun was directly overhead. They were perhaps a thousand paces from the peak. Without warning, the mountain shook violently, knocking them to the ground. A howling wind from the east blew against them. It was so strong Ko had to hold on to the trunk of an acacia bush or be blown away.

Just as suddenly as it began, it was over.

Jet pushed himself forward and after a long trek, made it to the very top of the mountain. "I'm here, sons of Set! What can you do to me now?" His voice echoed down the mountainside, bouncing back from the granite rocks and boulders.

"What can Set do to you, my Prince?" Merseruka asked. "Here is his answer." He pulled a dagger from his belt and stabbed the prince. The force of the blow was so great it knocked Jet down.

Ko rushed toward the general who was about to stab Jet again and struck him on the head with a rock. "Jet," he shouted. "Let me see."

"He cut my shoulder. I am going to kill him for that."

Ko helped Jet up and removed a brass chest and back piece of battle armor.

"If it hadn't been for these, I would have died high above the earth as the Setites promised."

"I don't understand it," his cousin said. "The general's not a son of Set. He bears no mark behind his ear or neck."

"Keep that rock handy, Ko. We may have to knock him out again before we get back down."

The return was easier, except they had to drag the general with them, happily knocking him out several more times.

The Crown Prince, in the King's name, made Captain Bakaa commander of the army until the king could appoint another, with promotion to Major. His first order was to advance the army north toward Byblos.

"We are leaving one thousand men here as I said, to work and protect the gold mine. We'll send more men and horses when we reach the sea," Bakaa said.

A great cheer went up from the warriors when the trumpeters sounded the advance. The army could finally put the strange mountain behind them. As they marched north, the land began to change. It was greener and more fertile the farther they marched and smelled rich and fecund.

Towns along the way, already defeated by the advancing Companies, were now home to the king's warriors who would remain there to keep order.

Bakaa's company, almost all seven hundred of them, faced no resistance, and so they enjoyed the rich bounty of the land.

The Sea Peoples, builders of merchant ships were traders on the Great Sea, and they did not resist the invaders. They had been defeated in an earlier battle by King Aha years ago. Bakaa's men took none of them prisoner since King Djed needed ships and their trade.

"It's been more than a year since we left Memphis," Ko said. "I left having seen sixteen summers, but now I have lived through seventeen and a half."

"An old man," Jet said. "We both will have to marry soon."

"I don't want to even think about it."

"Many of the royal family marry at twelve or thirteen, Cousin. By those standards we truly are old men."

Major Bakaa approached them at their camp one evening near the city of Byblos. "I will stay here with one company of the king's army until he appoints another General to be in charge. We must keep a tight grip on what we have won."

"We are ready to sail home, *Major*." Ko said.

"We need to send a message by pigeon tomorrow, so they will know we are alive and will be coming soon. How long a journey will it be from here?" Jet asked.

"We're almost as far north as we dare go, my friends. It will take three to four days to reach the mouth of our sacred river and then another four to Memphis."

"Does the king have a ship here?" Jet asked.

"Not yet, Highness, but you will sail on one of the finest galleys made today. These shipbuilders are masters of sea-worthy ships."

"What have you done with our fat assassin?" Ko asked.

"Ah, yes, remember, you said you couldn't understand why he attacked you, Highness. No one could find the mark on him or brand of the brotherhood, you said."

"Yes, it was true." Jet replied. "We found no mark on him."

"Not so, Crown Prince. On the arch of his left foot, there is a brand bearing Set's seal."

The two princes looked at each other in disbelief.

Bakaa laughed and continued. "No one looks at the soles of our feet. He wore his sandals all the time, and his aide said they never bathed him because he insisted on washing himself. He fooled us all."

Ko asked, "What will happen to him?"

"He will sail home with you as the king's prisoner. It is his majesty who will decide his fate. We know the king will give him what he deserves."

"I agree to that. If it hadn't been for my cousin making me wear the armor under my kaftan, I would have been Set's latest victim." He touched the bandage on his shoulder. "I'm glad it wasn't a deep wound, and the ointment is helping."

"What reward will you give him, Highness?"

Jet said, "If I let him marry my sister, he would become my brother-in-law."

"Merry? Young Merry? Surely not."

"I don't know if you've noticed, Cousin. She has become a beautiful woman."

Ko felt his face grow hot. It was true, and he had already noticed the last time he was at the palace. He looked away, so Jet wouldn't see him blushing and ordered another jug of beer.

The two princes sailed on the first ship filled with warriors from Horus Company. The cheering at the wharf was deafening and a crowd of Sea Peoples came to see what was causing their merriment.

After settling into the royal cabin, they walked out on deck. At the railing they watched overhead as long narrow banners the length of the ship waved their royal colors of blue and yellow. They were like long feathers on some great majestic bird.

As the wind filled the great sail it carried them away, and the city of Byblos grew smaller and smaller behind them.

Like the king's galleys, the Phoenicians used a large rectangular sail, and a method of using wooden pegs to lock the wooden planks in place making their ships watertight and secure. The one-hundred rowers were only needed if they were becalmed.

Jet leaned on the railing. "I don't know about you, but the motion of the waves is making me dizzy. I've never seen so much water."

"Let's sit in the breeze in front of the cabin," Ko suggested. After sharing a cool jar of beer, he felt good to be alive.

"I would have died if it were not for you, Cousin. I meant what I said to Bakaa. It would please me a great deal if you were to marry into our family. I know your father would be pleased, and I'm sure the king will be when he knows what you did for me."

"Jet, I do not deserve such an honor. Let's talk about it when we get home. Besides, the king may have already picked someone for Merry."

"I can change that. My life and succession to the throne should allow me to change his mind."

Ko closed his eyes and inhaled the rich sea air wafting over them. He imagined Princess Merry coming toward him, beautiful, walking with her head held high like a true royal. Perhaps he should give more thought to accepting his cousin's proposal after all.

20

"Where is he? I can't see him," the princess cried in frustration. She pushed the curtains of her carrying chair aside.

"Meowwrrrr?"

"No, Zee, he's not there."

"Remember who you are," Queen Nakhtneith said.

King Djer sat on his white horse waiting for the last lines to fall into place and be securely tied down. The crew lowered the gangway and unrolled a deep-blue carpet onto the pavement in front of his majesty.

Palace guards locked arms to form a protective barrier for the royal family to reach the ship.

A great roar welcomed the first troops to leave the vessel. All 250 men marched off and stood at attention. When the king moved his horse forward and dismounted, they fell onto one knee and saluted, fists across the chest. "Dee-jer! Dee-jer!" they shouted, repeating his name over and over.

His majesty raised his hand and spoke slowly, "Welcome back men of Horus Company, heroes of our great land. Your king greets you as do the people of Memphis."

Once again, the people—most of them wives and children bursting with pride—cheered for their warriors.

Walking down the carpet, the king made his way to the bottom of the gangway.

Kettle drums beat a long cadence and a silence fell over the crowd.

The Crown Prince stepped out of the cabin with his cousin and walked toward the main deck. A loud roar greeted him when he walked down the gangway with Prince Ako at his side. Trumpets blew a fanfare as the Crown Prince walked to the king, knelt and saluted.

In a voice loud and clear, the king said, "Welcome home, Victorious Warrior and Beloved Son of Horus." He extended his hand and his son took it and stood. The king turned him around so the crowd could see him.

There were cheers, clapping and some stomped their feet. "*Dee*-jet, *Dee*-jet," they chanted.

Ko waited at the beginning of the long carpet. Then, the tall figure of his father appeared next to the king. Prince Akhom walked around his majesty and made his way toward his son. They embraced and turned to face the king.

The king raised his hand for the two of them to approach.

"Welcome home, Prince Ako, Nephew of the king—Victorious Warrior and Son of Akhom, brother of the great Aha."

At the mention of Aha's name, hundreds of voices chanted, "We honor his name." Then they cheered for Ko, long and enthusiastically.

The king bent over slightly and whispered so only Ko could hear. "You have saved my son and brought him home. I will not forget."

Horses arrived for the two princes who saddled up and rode behind the king along the wide avenue to the palace.

As they passed the two golden carrying chairs, he saw Merry holding the cat in her arms. She smiled at him and gave a small wave. He bowed his head to

276 ~ William G. Collins

her and smiled. After a year and a half, to him she had grown more beautiful.

Leading the procession, priests of Horus and Ra lifted fragrant incense. When it reached Ko, the blue smoke made him sneeze. The scent of jasmine reminded him of his farewell to Merry over a summer and a half ago.

At the palace, servants escorted them to their apartments. But on the steps, old Ankhkahf, the chamberlain, took Ko aside.

"From what I hear, my boy, you have saved the kingdom."

"You embarrass me, Lord Chamberlain. What I did was in the king's name."

"As it should be. Horus go with you."

"And with you, my father's friend, and mine too, I pray."

Ko walked with his father the short distance home. At the door, his mother embraced him and wouldn't let him go.

"Nafrini," his father said. "Permit the boy to breathe."

After freshening up and a change of clothes, the family shared a delicious meal prepared by his mother's own hands. Later, the servants cleared the table as the family moved into their garden.

His mother said, "You look more and more like your father every day, but you've lost weight in the desert. I'll have to fatten you up."

Akhom frowned. "Let him be, Wife. He's trying to trim down to impress a certain lady at court."

"Oh?"

"Yes. Now Son, we have an important question for you." Akhom lowered his voice and asked, "What happened to you on the mountain?"

Ko took his time telling them everything. When he reached the part about the gold mine, they stopped him.

His father stood and paced about. "You were sealed in a black cave did you say? Only you and Djet were inside—no one else?"

"Yes, Father."

His parents looked at each other and nodded.

Ko said, "I heard your voices Father. Were you praying to the gods?"

"Indeed," Akhom replied. "And Horus answered, bless his name."

When Ko told them about General Merseruka's attempt to kill the Crown Prince, his father became angry. "Set take him to everlasting darkness."

Ko asked, "How did they get him to give up the names?"

Akhom smiled. "We were told he squealed like a stuck pig under torture."

"I'm glad then that we didn't kill him, but we wanted to. Jet will have that scar on his shoulder as a reminder of the man's treachery."

His mother spoke up. "Now tell us about the young lady who has captured your interest."

Ko wasn't sure this was the right time, but said, "Jet seeks to reward me for saving him by giving me his sister for wife. He is certain his father will approve."

Akhom rubbed his chin and then stood. "Of course, it is a great honor. Sons-in-law of the king can succeed to the throne. Would we ever have dreamed such a thing?"

Ko's mother studied her son's face for what seemed a long time. "Do you love her?" she asked.

"Mother, I don't really know her. She was becoming a woman when I left, even then I admired her for her beauty."

His father said, "She will soon have seen fifteen summers, my boy. You have another year at the military academy. By then, you will know if she is the one."

"Of course, Father. But I feel drawn to her."

Lady Nafrini stood. "Well, I will leave you two men to talk about fighting in the desert and that mysterious mountain."

After she'd gone, his father looked him in the eye. "How do you really feel about the princess?"

Ko sighed. "When I left Memphis a summer and a half ago, Merry appeared to have grown up quickly. It is true I am attracted to her, but I don't know why. I just am."

"The sages tell us that 'Love is one thing—knowledge is another. One is ruled by the heart, the other the head.' In these matters, my Son, the heart rules. You must learn all you can about her. Find out if she is the one you can spend the rest of your life with."

His father stood and stretched his back. "I encourage you to consider marrying her. You can go far in the army, that is true, but the way to power is with the royal family. We are already linked of course, but now, there would be a stronger blood tie—the most powerful of all."

"Good advice, my Lord, but I don't think I will sleep well tonight. Thinking about her makes me toss and turn all night."

"And so, you should," his father said. "Oh, to be your age again."

The next day, Major Bakaa came looking for Ko. He brought a horse for the prince. "The king has assembled his generals and officers at the military grounds. All the soldiers in this region are there and he wants us there too."

"What is it about, Major?" Ko asked.

"I don't know, we will know soon."

At the parade grounds, Ko and Bakaa joined the Crown Prince on the reviewing stand. The king gave a signal and the large kettle drums beat a call to attention. His majesty moved to the front and in a loud voice addressed the assembly.

"Men of the kingdom. We declare an end to the Followers of Set, god of darkness and hate. We order our troops into every town, village, farm and ship. Every citizen of the kingdom is to be examined. If any mark or tattoo with the symbol of Set is found, that person or persons is to be put to death. The bodies of every offender will be cut to pieces and thrown to the servants of Sobek in our sacred river. Death to the murderers of our king Aha and his queen, may we remember their names. Offer a silver coin to anyone who reports a suspected Setite."

The chamberlain walked forward. "This is the will of our king," he shouted.

The soldiers shouted, "So it is written, we will obey!"

His majesty hadn't finished. "We also declare that every temple of Set, every shrine, every altar will be torn down, and every statue destroyed. Those who try to hide or give shelter to the priests or priestesses will receive the same punishment."

The chamberlain then brought out the royal flail and shepherd's crook and the king held them in his hands. He said, "This is the law. Let it be written. Let it be done."

The soldiers cheered and beat their shields with their swords.

Major Bakaa walked with Ko and said, "I am leaving tomorrow with a patrol for Thinis, and you are to come with us. We are to round up the Setites you discovered there. We hope the Jackal will be in the last group to be arrested. He's eluded us so far. Jet will travel with us."

"Gladly. It will be a pleasure to see the motherless sons suffer," Ko replied.

As they saddled up, Bakaa said, "You must show us how to find the ancient shrine you told us about over a summer ago."

"Of course, but no one will be there, Major. The Jackal and his men fled the ruin after killing two of my men. Using the river, they escaped into the darkness."

"That may no longer be true, Highness," Bakaa said. "During his painful interrogation, Merseruka revealed that the leaders *had* returned to Thinnis. We want to catch them in their lair."

"Excellent news, Major," Ko said.

When they reached the palace garrison, Jet joined them and Bakaa told him what he had shared with his cousin.

Jet asked, "How would you go about capturing them, Ko?"

"In the middle of the night." He slapped a mosquito that landed on his forehead, scratched the spot, before continuing. "That's when they have their secret ceremonies. While they're meeting, we must block the tunnel that leads below at both ends. Give the command and we rush in and arrest them. They won't be there in the day time."

Bakaa nodded. "Then that's what we'll do."

Jet asked, "How can we be sure if they are there?"

Ko said, "An excellent question, brother toad. You and I will visit the family I met who live on the street near the ruin. They can tell us when the followers of the dark god will be there."

"Very well," Bakaa said. "We'll camp nearby, somewhere out of sight and await the signal."

It took them a day and a half to sail to Thinis. The princes went with Bakaa's men to a small farm behind the street leading to the ruined shrine. They hid in the barn along with their horses. The farmer would watch the animals that night when the men went on foot to the house.

Having changed into ordinary tunics, Ko and Jet walked down the dirt street to the house Ko had visited before. When he knocked on the clay bricks bordering the curtained door, the woman came out and recognized him at once. She bowed and waited for him to speak.

"Please stand, good woman. We come asking your help. We must know if the followers of the dark god have returned to the ruin and when they meet."

She listened to his words and nodded. "Tonight, Great One. They meet every ten nights, and this is the tenth."

"Thank Horus," Ko sighed. He sat on the old bench near the doorway. "We need to send for the men."

Jet said, "I'll bring them. You wait here."

When the prince had gone, the woman said, "Come inside out of the heat, my Lord."

Dusting off a chair, Ko sat down. Unsanitary odors made him rub his nose. She returned with a cup of water and slice of bread. It wasn't long before Jet returned with Bakaa and the rest of the men.

"Everyone, to the back of the house," the major ordered. "Settle under the palms and rest. We need to be patient. They may not come at all."

The woman held the youngest child in her arms. "Oh, they'll come, my Lords. They meet without fail." She spoke to Ko as if he was in charge. "I'll take my children to my neighbor. She'll put them to bed. We've all been fearful for our children. I'm glad you've come back."

"If Horus is willing, good woman, we will put an end to your fears," Ko assured her.

Bakaa's men would have a long wait until the middle of the night. They took turns watching the road, while others dozed in the back. Dishes clanking and the nearby neighbor's conversations soon faded, and all oil lamps extinguished. It was Ko and Jet's turn to watch for the Setites.

Light from a half-moon brightened the way to the ruins and Jet suddenly poked Ko's arm. Two men approached and passed the house. Hoods covered their heads and more men followed. Ko counted fifteen and prayed that one of them would be the Jackal. He couldn't be sure he would remember what the man looked like.

A cold breeze sent a chill into the house and Ko felt the gooseflesh on his arms. A lone figure walked down the street. He turned toward the house and for an instant, the pale moonlight lit up his face.

Ko recognized the man and his heart beat faster. The Jackal!

No one moved except for the man on the road who continued to the shrine.

Ko whispered, "Major, tell the men we're ready. We must move quickly and block both ends of the tunnel. I'll show them to you. Walk lightly, vibrations can be felt underground."

Bakaa nodded, gave the order, and he and the princes led the advance toward the ruin.

Placing his men at each end of the tunnel, Bakaa motioned for them to advance down the steps into the cave. What followed was pandemonium. The major ordered his men to draw their weapons, and they immediately engaged in hand-to-hand fighting.

Ko struck down two men and others fell from the blows of Bakaa's men. It was a short engagement and the soldiers subdued those still alive. The only light was a small oil lamp that still burned.

Ko shouted, "Here he is, Major—killer of babies—and his majesty's soldiers. This is the Jackal and leader of the abomination of Set. The king will want this one alive."

The Jackal shouted, "Spawn of the cursed Aha," but Jet struck him on the mouth, knocking him down. "Tie him and assign four men to watch his every move. Gag him too, we don't want to hear any more of his filth."

Bakaa and his men retrieved their horses and marched the prisoners to a ship that would take them back to Memphis.

Ko's father learned of their arrival and went to meet them at the palace stockade. "You have found him, thank the gods," Akhom said. "We now have more than a hundred members of the evil brotherhood. We will destroy the followers for good this time. His majesty is pleased and prays that his reign will now be free of their evil influence."

"How will the king punish them, Father?" Ko asked.

"We will have to wait and see until after the great celebration of your victories in the desert. It will be a glorious day."

The morning after their return, Ko heard his mother enter his room and pull back the curtains. "Good morning, mighty warrior."

Ko grumbled something but turned over and refused to open his eyes. He had been troubled by many dreams, most of which were of a certain young woman.

"There's a guard waiting for you in the front room, Ko. Wash quickly and get dressed. Your father has already left for the ceremony and I am leaving to join him."

"Gods! I was to meet with the king before it starts. Let me dress."

When his mother had gone, he washed quickly, pulled on a clean kilt and ran his fingers through his hair. Straightening the necklace of the falcon-god Merry gave him, he ran out of the house.

At the palace, the chamberlain scowled at him. "There you are at last. He's inside."

A guard opened the door to the dressing chamber next to the Audience Hall, and let him in.

"Ah, Ko, I was about to order the guards to fetch you. Good. Sit over there while they finish with me."

"Majesty, I overslept. Forgive me."

"I want to talk to you about my daughter."

Ko's face grew warm, and he hoped the king wouldn't notice.

The king frowned. "My advisors tell me I cannot allow this marriage."

21

The king adjusted his double crown and turned to face his nephew. "Jet promised something he had no power or permission to grant. We are not related by blood but by royal decree. And you are a lowly army trainee."

"I know, Great King. He is like a brother to me and this was his way of showing his gratitude, I know that. But I love her, Majesty, and I know she loves me."

Pharaoh smiled. "It is I who decide Ko, I alone. After consideration of my counselors' advice, and in speaking with the queen, we agree to your marriage with our daughter. And Jet made me swear that I would agree to it."

"Thank you, Majesty. You must know that Princess Merneith has grown into a beautiful woman before our eyes. I was struck by the change when I bade her, and the queen farewell the day we sailed to Awen."

The king nodded. "You will be returning there to finish your military training with my son, won't you?"

"Yes, Great One, with your permission."

"Granted, of course, you know that." The king paused while the dressers placed the last gold necklace around his neck.

The king smiled. "I will announce your betrothal this morning. We will be proud to have you marry our daughter. Just don't get yourself killed during the rest of your training."

"You honor me and my family, Majesty. Of course, I will have the protection of the Crown Prince during training. We will look after each other."

"Then you should do well. Now go and prepare yourself for the ceremony."

After the Audience Hall filled with courtiers and other invited guests, the Lord Chamberlain struck the polished granite floor with his staff for silence. "Behold Queen Nakhneith, Daughter of Isis, the Great Royal Wife and Mother of the Crown Prince. Bow down and be in awe!"

A trumpet fanfare echoed throughout the hall. The invited guests prostrated themselves, toward the queen.

She walked majestically, head held high and her chin out. Ko thought his sister, at thirty summers, never looked as beautiful as she did at that moment. Her long, pleated gown was the color of the sky, and gathered tightly under her bosom, made the material billow around her like the morning mist. She walked up the three steps and stood in front of her golden throne.

Ankhkahf declared in a loud voice. "Behold Crown Prince Djet, Son of Horus, First Son of King Djed, Father of our Land."

The courtiers remained on the floor as the prince walked toward the front and stood to the right of his father's throne.

Now, in his loudest voice, Ankhkahf said, "Bow low and be in awe of His Majesty, King Djed, Beloved Son of Horus, Ruler of the Two Kingdoms of Upper and Lower Kemet, Father of the Crown Prince and Ruler of the Land."

A much longer fanfare announced his arrival.

He strode forth deliberately, not looking to the right or left. Climbing the three steps he extended his hand to his queen, helping her take her place. He turned and sat on the larger of the two golden thrones.

The chamberlain tapped the staff three times, and the courtiers stood and bowed their heads respectfully to the king.

Inside the Great Hall, standing in front of the large doors, Ko fidgeted as he stood next to Major Bakaa waiting for their summons. From where he and the officer stood at the back of the hall, the royals appeared bathed in sunlight which streamed through narrow open windows. It focused everyone's attention on the king and queen. Ko felt uncomfortable in this kind of gathering. He took some comfort in the Major's nervous habit of continually putting his hand on the hilt of his sword and then removing it.

Finally, Ankhkahf called their names and they walked in side by side. At the front, they knelt and saluted their majesties.

The king stood. "Stand, Heroes of the land."

The court burst into applause and Ko sensed his face turning red. He glanced toward the courtiers in the front row and his eyes met those of Merry standing in front of her royal chair. She smiled at him and he quickly looked front.

"Major Bakaa, Son of Sahura, for leading the Army of the North and for the capture of the traitor

Merseruka, we award the Gold of Valor and promote you to the rank of General. You will take command of the Army of the North."

Roaring applause filled the room as the king took the gold necklace from a box held by the chamberlain and placed it around the officer's neck. He then turned him around to face the assembly who clapped enthusiastically.

The king then turned to his nephew. "Prince Ako, Son of Akhom our beloved Uncle, stand forth."

Ko took a step forward and stood at attention.

"We award this Gold of Valor for saving the life of the Crown Prince, and for arresting the disgraced leader of the army. For the discovery of the gold mine which will enrich our people and land, we also express our gratitude."

The chamberlain brought another box and the king took out the necklace with a Deben of the precious metal suspended on it, bearing the king's throne name.

It felt heavy as it lay on Ko's chest. He looked up and returned the king's smile before stepping back.

The court applauded the two men as they turned and were about to leave.

"Prince Ako," the king called him back. "Remain with us."

King Djed walked toward his daughter and reached for her hand. He led her back to the front of the thrones. Facing the court, he said, "We announce today the betrothal of our Beloved Merneith to Prince

Ako." He took the young man's hand and put Merry's hand in his.

The courtiers roared their approval.

Ko smiled at the princess, whose cheeks turned pink. She smiled the broadest smile and winked at him.

"Kiss her, my son," the king encouraged.

Ko turned to the princess and kissed her chastely on the cheek to more cheering by the court.

Afterwards, outside in the king's gardens, servants served beer, wine and pastries.

Surprisingly, Ko resented the crowd because he was unable to spend any time with the princess. Congratulations on their betrothal meant the well-wishers demanded her attention. He chose to remain with his parents until they excused themselves and they walked home together.

In the morning, Bakaa the new general, called for Ko to join him at the place of execution. The followers of Set, now bound and gagged, were put on wagons and transported to the river's edge south of the city.

"Where is the Jackal—murderer of children?" Ko asked Bakaa.

"He will be fed to the crocodiles last, Prince."

Jet overheard him. "The servants of Sobek will eat well today. But even this is too good a punishment for them."

Bakaa said, "They've had their eyes burned out. His majesty ordered it because they love darkness more than light. He wanted to prepare them for the everlasting obscurity of the underworld."

Ko shuddered. "A horrible punishment, General, but they deserve it."

"I agree," Jet said. "Especially Merseruka."

A contingent of royal guards marched on each side of the king as he rode his horse to the platform built for him to oversee the executions. Dismounting, he motioned for Bakaa, his son and Ko to join him on the platform.

Ko hesitated at first, but then climbed the steps and stood next to his majesty.

Water on the surface of the sacred river roiled with the movement of so many crocodiles eager for what was about to happen. Fed at the same spot so many times, their jaws opened and closed as the scent of the prisoners reached them.

The king raised his hand, and when he lowered it, the first five prisoners were thrown into the water. The screams of the condemned men made Ko's stomach turn. He wanted to close his eyes to the carnage as more prisoners met their doom but feared offending the king.

After what felt like an eternity, the Jackal, the leader, disappeared in a swirl of blood. The last to die was Merseruka. Stripped of his clothing, his eyes now blackened sockets he cursed the king before hitting the water.

"Horus is good," the king proclaimed in a louder voice.

The guards and men on the platform shouted back the declaration.

Ko finally turned away, praying his knees wouldn't give out as he followed the king away from the place of death.

The king said, "Executions are taking place throughout the country. By Set's buttocks, let us pray this will be an end to all Setites!"

When the victory and betrothal celebrations finally ended, it was time for Ko and his cousin to return to their training at Awen. At sunup, they boarded a ship and stood at the railing waving to the crowd of family and friends. The royal galley's rectangular sail caught the morning breeze carrying it out into the fast current that would take them north. Once again, narrow ship-length banners of the royal colors fluttered in the breeze, announcing to the world there were royals on board.

"It doesn't feel right heading back to the Academy without our friend Bakaa," Ko said.

"I agree. As much as we made his life difficult, he proved an excellent officer."

"I hope in a year we will have learned some of his leadership skills."

Jet moved closer to his cousin. "Won't it be hard to be away from your betrothed for a year, royal toad?"

Ko turned away from him and stared at green farmlands sailing past. "I didn't have much time with her, brother. I'm not even sure I should share with you how I feel about her."

"Oh, I see. I should be indignant that you would have amorous thoughts about my sister?"

"That's enough, Jet, or I'll tell the king about your little dalliance with Bektamun. I was with you in Thebes, remember?"

"Fine, but I regret nothing. She's still an amazing woman."

"Yes, and at least ten summers your senior."

Jet tried to hit him, but Ko easily ran along the deck to the helm.

The captain of the ship stopped them. "I will have no fighting on my ship, young Lords."

"Agreed, Captain, but the Crown Prince is high-spirited today."

"Very well, Highness." The man studied the sky and the passing landscape. "We will be in Awen in three days if the gods are willing,"

"Thank you, Captain. We do promise to behave."

Ko walked to the bow and inhaled the wonderful fragrances of the river. He crossed his arms and remembered Merry's kiss before he came aboard. He promised her he would write as often as he could, and they agreed to use special words to make sure their letters really came from each other.

Returning to his cabin, he stretched out on his bed. A new carved ivory comb rested on the small stand by it, a gift from his mother before their departure. Next to it stood a small beautifully sculpted alabaster bust of his betrothed—a gift from his sister, the queen.

"It will remind you of Merry," she told him, "and might help you stay true to her on those lonely nights."

The door opened, and Jet asked, "What about a game of Senet?"

"All right, but I beat you every time," Ko said. "But let's play outside on deck."

Jet laughed. "You'll not stand a chance this time." He turned to go and saw the bust of his sister. "Where did that come from? That's from my mother's room."

"Is it? I didn't know. Your mother gave it to me before we sailed."

Jet walked out of the cabin. "Come on."

Back at the Academy, their old comrades cheered the royals when they entered the barracks.

"Welcome back, chiefs among toads," Babu said, laughing and shaking their hands.

Ko liked being with his friends again. They treated him like one of them.

Major Menkhaf greeted them with enthusiasm.

Surprisingly, it was also good to be back to a routine that didn't require much thought.

Several days later, the major called an assembly in the common room and announced a new yet old mission. "Merchant caravans are still being attacked. The governor has asked us again to help. You're all archers, swordsmen so the thieves will not stand a chance."

"Ko will be our sergeant this time," Menkhaf announced.

Titles meant nothing at the Academy, whether for sons of noble families or the ruling class—all were treated the same.

Later, at archery practice, Jet said, "Sergeant, what is your plan to destroy these bandits?"

Ko scowled. "There is no plan, soldier. The major is waiting for more information from the officer of the city garrison."

Jet stretched out on the soft grass. "I was only going to suggest they could be desert dwellers who are trying to terrorize the region."

Ko sat on an old wooden bench. "I have thought of that, too, brother. What if they used the curved swords we saw at the great mountain?"

"Gods, Ko. We would be at a great disadvantage."

They sat in silence a few moments until Ko said, "We must ask the city commander if they have captured desert fighters in the past. They may have some of their swords we could train with and use them against the thieves."

Jet said, "Brilliant. I'll go find out." He jumped up and left the archery field.

A week later, Major Menkhaf, Ko and their brigade of twenty warriors left the city. Four of their swordsmen had trained with the curved desert swords.

That first night, half of them stood watch. Two days later, they met a caravan heading for Awen.

Ko asked the caravan master, "Can we travel with you? We could hide in your wagons and defend you if attacked."

"It would be reassuring, Sergeant," the merchant said. "We are hauling valuable spices and incense for the Temple of the Sun in Awen. It's worth a fortune."

"You are three days from the city. Let us camp with you tonight. If you have an extra kaftan or two, we will disguise ourselves."

"Agreed, but we don't anticipate any trouble."

Ko said, "Let us pray the gods agree with you."

After they'd settled down, Menkhaf's men kept watch from beneath the wagons and behind large boulders.

In the darkness, Ko strained to see, as the lonely cries of a shrike pierced the night.

Jet was on the other side of the wagon and two of the men with kopesh swords were crouched under it near him.

In the middle of the night as the fire burned low, the bandits attacked.

They rushed into camp forcing the men of the caravan to lie down by the fire. When they attempted to remove merchandise from the wagons, Ko gave the order to rush in. Arrows flew at the thieves killing three of them. Ko's men ran toward the others, engaging them with desert swords.

The thieves were easily dispatched and the last one standing fought hand-to-hand with Ko. The man was strong and pushed the prince toward one of the wagons.

Ko lost his footing and fell, giving the thief the chance to thrust his sword down, slicing into Ko's chest. The prince cried out in pain and Jet rushed forward, running the bandit through.

Ko groaned. "Help me, brother."

One of their brigades brought a torch from the fire so they could see.

Ko first felt and then saw the blood running down his chest.

Jet yelled, "Pressure!" He tore a large piece from his kilt and pressed the cloth down on the wound. "Carry him closer to the fire."

Ko gritted his teeth. He began to feel dizzy but grabbed Jet's hand,

Jet squeezed it hard. "We will get you to a physician, brother."

It was the last words Ko heard as he passed out.

22

Slivers of sunlight touched Ko's face and he opened his eyes. A terrible pain burned in his chest. "Where am I?" he asked, his speech slow and slurry.

"Easy, brother. You might undo the stitches. The physician has sown you up."

The door of the room opened, and a distinguished nobleman approached the bed.

"Ah, my patient is awake. That is a good sign."

Jet said, "What are his chances, my Lord?"

"Well, the cut was clean, and thanks to the curved blade of the bandit, it didn't go deep enough to hit his heart or lungs. The fever will be our concern. Douse him with pails of water to keep him cool. Change his bandages each day."

Ko groaned again. "The caravan? Everything lost?"

Jet pulled up the chair beside the cot. "We defeated them and captured seven, Sergeant Ko. The governor is very pleased."

"Drink this," the healer ordered his patient.

"Where are we?" Ko mumbled.

"On a ship headed for Memphis, brother. The king will insist only the royal physicians at the palace care for you."

Ko's eyes grew heavy and he drifted off into a painless sleep.

When he came to again, he found a woman sitting by his bed.

"Water," he whispered.

She handed him a cup and helped him drink.

"Who?" he asked, trying to focus. "Merry? No, it can't be."

"Go back to sleep, brave one," the princess said. "You are home in my apartment."

Having heard them talking, the physician entered. "Good, Highness. The fever has broken, Ko, and you are out of danger."

"Thank the gods," Merry said.

"How long?" Ko asked.

"It's been four days," the princess answered. "You had a very high fever, but you survived it. Horus be praised."

"Physician," Ko called to the healer.

"Yes, Highness?"

"The wound?"

"It is healing nicely, Prince. The sword cut through several muscles but was deflected by your necklace of the god Horus. Two of your ribs were nicked, but you should make a good recovery."

Ko reached for the medallion on his necklace and held it up. "Merry and Horus. Who can beat them? Then I should be all right, Physician?"

"Yes, the man said, "but. . . "

"But?"

"Any more soldiering is out of the question, I'm afraid. Your injury limits your use of the muscles on your right side. I'm sorry."

Ko swallowed hard and bit his lip to keep tears from filling his eyes. He gritted his teeth as another wave of pain hit him. He thought of his father's disappointment that his son wouldn't be an officer. Why had the gods done this to him? He closed his eyes and feigned sleep, hoping Merry would leave, and she did.

Later, when his parents and sister, the queen, came to visit, they did not speak about what his injury could mean for his future. He was glad to escape thinking about it through pain killers and medicine that induced sleep.

A week later, Ko was able to sit in the family room. His constant companion, his betrothed, took care of him day and night. It was the closest they had ever been. He found her to be an intelligent, pleasant companion, and was most eloquent in discussing subjects in which, he too, was interested.

He was honored by several visits from his sister and the king who insisted they would do everything to help him get well.

Zeezee the cat never left him, sleeping on his bed and nudging him with her head. He found the cat's contented purring helped him sleep.

A few days passed, and his father insisted his son return to the family home much to Merry's dismay.

It still took a month for him to feel himself again. He insisted his father help him go to the palace to visit the princess. It was for the celebration of her name day—the fifteenth summer of her birth day, and he brought her a gift.

"Oh, what is it?" she asked him, sounding pleased he brought her something.

She opened the small box and found a beautiful thin yellow cloth. She took it out carefully and found something inside it. "Oh," she said again as she lifted out a gold necklace and pendant. She examined it closely. "It's my name. It's beautiful. Thank you, Ko."

"I had the goldsmith make it especially for today. It is from the gold of the great mountain. The gods of the desert winds have kissed it."

She walked over and embraced him, careful not to hurt his chest or side.

Ko's body reacted to her closeness and he thrilled to the passion of her kiss. He pulled her closer and they held each other, not wanting to let go.

Her brother intruded. "Princess, you have other guests who have also brought gifts."

Ko let her go and turned away, so Jet could not see the color of his face.

"What's the matter, Ko? I'm not fooled. You really are alive, aren't you? I was afraid that wound to your chest killed your heart. But there is hope for you after all."

Ko laughed and turned to face him. "I want to be serious for a moment, Cousin. I never thanked you for saving my life. I realize now how close to death I came." His voice trembled with emotion. "While I may never be an officer in your army, when you become king, I want to be at your side if you allow it."

"You can thank me first of all, by marrying my sister and moving her into the house the king has been building for you both."

"I didn't realize he was building one. It will be pleasant to be on our own, but near friends and family." Jet nodded, and Ko added, "I will speak to him about the marriage, I promise."

Early one morning, Ko awoke to find his father watching him from the chair next to the bed. He sat up. "What is it, Father? What is wrong?"

"Nothing my boy. The chamberlain is in the garden and has asked to speak with you."

"Ankhkahf? What could he want?"

"Get dressed. I'll tell him you will come outside."

Ko saw his father's expression change when he saw again the large bandages covering his son's right side and chest. He turned away and walked into the garden.

Ko swung his legs to the edge of the bed and stood slowly, steadying himself to get his balance. His mother saw him leave his room and offered her arm.

"Thank you, my Lady. I really feel like I need to learn how to walk again."

"Be strong, my Son. You are doing well."

When they entered the garden, the elderly Ankhkahf stood and walked toward them.

"Lady Nafrini. Allow me to help this young hero," he said.

"We are honored by your visit, Lord Chamberlain. I leave my son in good hands." She smiled and allowed Ankhkahf to help her son walk to a stone bench in the shade.

Ko sat quietly, almost out of breath from the exertion. He was pleased the elderly man waited until he was composed enough to speak.

"May I call you, Ko, young man? I've known you since the day you were born."

"Of course, my Lord."

"Good. Ko, I have come on a very personal mission. The gods have been good to me and have allowed me seventy summers. But his majesty needs a chamberlain who is strong and powerful."

"I understand."

Ankhkahf leaned closer. "I want to propose to the king that you be named Chamberlain when the gods take me."

Ko wasn't sure he heard correctly and that it was not something the medicine was creating in his mind. "I don't understand."

"I know you wanted to be an officer like your father. The physician is convinced your body will not allow that to happen. Mine is an honored position, second only to the Crown Prince. I work closely with his majesty on everything. It will allow you to serve the king, my prince, and the family you now love *and* admire. We can work together as you learn what all there is to do."

Ko was silent a long time and he could see his lack of a response was troubling the chamberlain. "Dear friend," Ko began. "I am so honored by this suggestion. Will you let me consider it while I regain my strength? I will give my answer soon."

Ankhkahf smiled back. "Excellent. That pleases me. Say nothing to anyone except for family." He stood and offered his hand. "Can I help you back indoors?"

"No, I'll rest here awhile. Thank you, Lord Chamberlain."

When the elder statesman had gone, Ko took a deep breath—even though doing so hurt his side. He let it out slowly. "Chamberlain," he said aloud. "Who would have imagined it?"

Eight weeks passed, and Ko's wounds healed nicely.

The royal wedding of Prince Ko and Princess Merry took place at the magnificent temple of Horus.

The high priest held a golden bowl of incense and paced out deliberate steps in a prescribed pattern around the young couple. A chorus of priests chanted songs dedicated to Ra, the companion god of Horus. Their deep voices echoed down the aisles of the great temple. High above, the golden images of the god helping Kemet's people, reflected the morning light.

Seated near the altar, the king and queen smiled approvingly at the proceedings.

Akhom and Ko's mother stood to the right of the couple, as witnesses before the court and the gods that they approved the union.

Ko's bride was resplendent in a long pleated rose-colored gown, which moved with the gentle breezes inside the holy place. Her servants arranged her hair up on the top of her head as he had first seen her two summers ago. Golden threads woven through the hair gave the appearance of a crown.

Green malachite eye shadow accented the slivers of green in her eyes, and her lips glistened with the color of red pomegranate begging to be kissed. She held his hand so tightly he thought she might break one of the bones.

Ko wore a white kilt, touched with strands of gold thread. His bare chest's only adornment was the golden necklace Merry had given him, which saved his life. He wore his long scar proudly and without shame.

He felt something brush against his shin and glanced down to see Zee looking up at him. She began to purr so loudly, he could feel the vibrations tickling his ankle.

"Your Highness," the priest called to him, bringing him back to the moment.

He knew it was time for him and his bride to present their gifts to the god. Together, they picked up a golden platter of precious jewels and approached the gigantic sculpture of the falcon-god. Merry then took their gift and placed it on the stone altar at the statue's base.

"Hear our prayer, Great Horus," Ko began. "Bless our union this day, and may we have many children to grow and honor your name."

The high priest placed incense on the altar and its sweet fragrance filled the sanctuary.

The young couple bowed their heads to the god before returning to their places in front of the main altar.

The chorus of priests circled the couple, and the high priest led them out to the entrance of the temple. Their guests followed the procession outside, following instructions from the royal guards as to where they should stand to greet newlyweds.

Everyone approached and wished them well. The bride's mother carried Merry's cat and walked with her husband to the carrying chair. The king mounted his white horse and waited for the guards to take their positions.

His father and mother came out of the temple last and hugged the newlyweds. Akhom was too moved to trust his voice, but Lady Nafrini said, "You are blessed by the gods. We know that. You have survived attacks to your person, Ko, and beaten the gods of the desert winds. This new step as Chamberlain will also be blessed by Great Horus."

Merry embraced her mother-in-law, and Ko kissed his sister on the cheek. "Thank you both for being here for me. I am a son most blessed. Horus be with you as well."

He kissed Merry again as they stood alone on the top step of the temple. The guards restrained the crowds who cheered the young couple and threw flowers toward them.

In their new home, their time of honey and fermented mead brought the two lovers together in the pleasant experience of intimacy. Careful of Ko's scars, they were able to experience the joys of physical union time and time again.

After another month, friends and members of the royal family made him welcome at court, but he missed the crown prince who had returned to Awen to complete his training. Ko insisted on training with his sword and felt his muscles compensating for those injured in the attack. His father was amazed at how well he'd progressed in his training.

One day, when the king and chamberlain finished in the Hall of Audiences, Ko met Lord Ankhkahf in the hallway. "May we speak, Lord Chamberlain, or is this a bad time?"

"Of course, my boy. Your words are most welcome. Walk with me to my study. It isn't far."

When they were seated in the room, Ko couldn't believe how many scrolls filled the shelves on all four sides.

"You appear well, young man."

"I am grateful to the gods, my Lord. I practice with my sword each day and the muscles are remembering how to move. It is painful, but I am making progress."

"Good. The king told me the other day how well you were doing."

"Oh?" Ko smiled knowing his wife had kept her father informed of his progress. "I have an answer for you, Honored One. If the king will have me, I would be humbled to learn from you about how to be a good chamberlain."

Ankhkahf stood. "Ah, I'm so glad. This calls for wine." He clapped his hands and a servant, ordered to bring a jar of wine, returned with it and two cups. The elderly man raised his wine. "To our new Chamberlain. Lord Ako, Nephew of the King."

Ko touched his cup to Ankhkahf's and said, "May Horus approve of this humble prince and help me be as good as you have been to the king."

On his father's most recent visit, Akhom said, "I am proud you have decided to be chamberlain, my son. Soldiers—there are many, but very few chamberlains. Your name will be etched in stone for all time along with Djet and the royal family."

Eleven cycles of the moon passed, and after the festival of the Great Inundation, Prince Djet, now captain, came home for the celebrations.

Ko and Merry invited him to spend time with them at their villa. The two cousins took up where they had left off a year ago. Ko admired the changes in his friend. He was taller, more confident and had a much more pleasant disposition. He was almost a different person.

"Who is this?" Jet exclaimed when his sister carried out a newborn.

Merry handed the baby to her brother who was uncertain how to hold it. He was all hands and seemed fearful of crushing the infant in his arms.

Ko said, "This is, Dewen—*he who brings the water*. We call him Den."

Jet kissed the baby and quickly handed him back to Merry. "I could make some stupid remark about babies always bring water, but I know you are honoring Hapi, god of the river."

Ko punched his cousin on the shoulder but was forced to burst out laughing.

When the baby was asleep, the three friends walked to the back garden where a large statue of Horus stood. It was as tall as three men and situated on a rise of the earth. From there they could see the sacred river and breathe in the wonderful scents of their rich, fertile land.

Ko heard a familiar sound and looked up. "Now that is a sight from our past, brother. When we were little, do you remember? We stood on that dune at Abydos where your grandfather Aha was buried."

"I remember, Ko. It is a falcon and is a sign of Horus' blessing."

As they watched, another falcon joined the first and the raptors called to each other as they circled higher and higher.

A warm desert wind blew past them, catching Merry's hair and she turned and laughed.

Ko said, "It is as if the gods of the desert winds also want to assure us that all will be well."

The majestic birds flew higher and higher and disappeared into the golden rays of the sun.

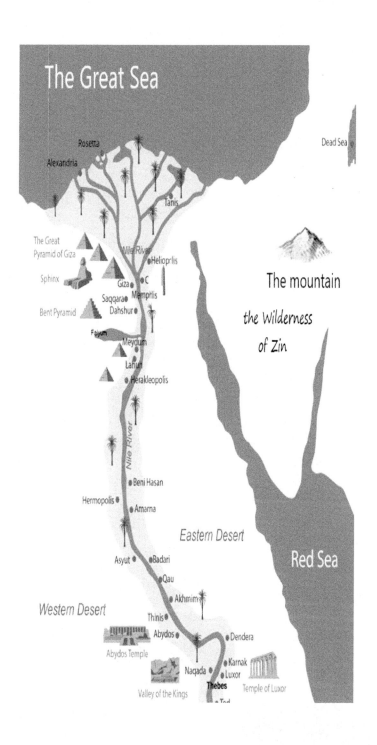

Made in the USA
Monee, IL
02 June 2020

32393296R00177